I0451233

by

Trenette Wilson

Trenette Wilson

The Designer's Daughter

What do you do…When the Perfect Love Hurts?

Copyright © *2010 Trenette Wilson.*

All rights reserved. No portion of this book can be reproduced or transmitted in any form or by any means, electronic, or mechanical, including photocopying, recording, or by an information storage and retrieval system, without written permission from the author, except for the inclusion of brief quotations in a review.

Published by
UrbanGirlz Publishing Company
P.O. Box 3641, Cedar Hill, Texas 75104
www.urbangirlz.org

ISBN 10: 0615397220
ISBN 13: 9780615397221

TEEN/YOUNG ADULT FICTION/SUSPENSE/RELATIONSHIPS

Library of Congress Cataloging-In-Publication Data is available from the publisher.

This book is available for bulk discounts. For more information contact: info@urbangirlz.org or call 1.800.291.6492.

Dedication

This book is dedicated to those who have found themselves hopelessly in love while standing on the other side of a raised fist or outstretched hand.

May these words help you to **LIVE**!

.

Trenette Wilson

Acknowledgments

I would like to thank my husband who is my greatest supporter and investor, I could not be a writer without you. I would also like to thank my children for being wonderful and a blessing and gift from God. Finally, thank you to my family and friends for bearing with me during the writing and editing process

I would also like to thank the following people who helped me throughout the publishing process.

Editing
Miriam Glover, Mavis Caldwell

Review Readers
Melody Nixon, Keke Perez, Demetric Taylor, Sophie Ford, Chermera McGhee, Karen Griggsby

Cover Design
Landa Morgan – Nfuxion Design Company

Cover Photographer
Issac Freeman

Promo Photographer
Daniel Smiley

Table of Contents

Chapter One: The Commission

I was sitting in my car trying to adjust the radio while my husband, Omar, went into the convenience store to get some candy for me. He was on the hunt for the all elusive 'Peanut Patty' that I had to eat at the end of each day. He wasn't happy because we'd already been to three stores with no luck.

He pulled into one final convenience store, warning me that this would be the last store he planned to check. We were home visiting both our families for the first time in about eight years. I was fiddling with the radio station, when I looked up and my heart skipped a beat! I slid down as low as I could in my seat, as I strained to see if it was him. I mean he had aged, but oh my goodness, it was him. My old boyfriend, Craig Lyles! I felt a tremor run through my body as my mind rushed back to the very first time we met…

It all began the summer I graduated from Winfro Girl's Academy. My mom, Renee Boyd, is an interior designer to the stars and professional athletes.

Since I can remember, she worked long hours and I had to stay with grandparents and nannies, but I loved her anyway. She's mom and the most glamorous person I know.

We'd just come from the flea market shopping for the oldest stuff she could find.

"Don't you just love this?" she'd ask every time she found something cracked and rusted.

I kept telling her everything looked old.

She seemed happy because she kept turning around while swirling her awful dusty cloth bags.

"Mom, you're going to give me an allergy attack with all that dust," I protested.

On the drive home, she talked about all the work she had to do and how glad she was that I was finally going to college. I was used to hearing that all my life, I know I hold momma back.

As we pulled into the driveway, one of her favorite songs came on the radio.

"See, that's what I'm talking about, that's real music," she began turning up the radio as loud as it would go and singing at the top of her voice.

"That song is old mom," I said getting out of the car to get our bags. She didn't care about my opinion because she got out and danced so hard I thought she was going to pull something.

"Momma, that's just wrong on so many levels," I said laughing so hard tears started rolling down my face.

She continued to sing and dance all the way into the house. Just as she began to explain how all dances started with the mashed potatoes, her telephone rang.

"Renee Boyd Interior Designs," she said unlocking the door running to put the telephone on speaker.

"That's cute. Got something I want you to hear," said the voice on the telephone. It was my Aunt Sandra. She was my mother's agent and also my godmother.

My mom and Aunt Sandra were college roommates and since I was born there's always been Aunt Sandra. My mom says she's the coolest white girl she knows. I think she's the smartest.

"Hello, Sandra, this is Darron Lyles, we love the specs Renee sent over. My wife and I agree; we want to hire her for the house here in L.A. Talk to you later to work out the details. Price is not an issue."

"Did you hear him just hire you to decorate his 15 million dollar, 12 bedroom house?" shouted Aunt Sandra.

Mom just fell to her knees.

"I told him you'd be available to consult with him and his wife Sydney, tomorrow around 11:00 a.m. where you will sign the contract with all the bells and whistles including car service."

"I'm so overwhelmed right now," mom began.

"Thank you so much Sandra, you're such a dear friend," mom sobbed. "I love you girl. This is it! What we've worked so hard for, thank you so much, this couldn't have happened without you!"

Mom continued jumping up and doing some kind of dance where she ran in place and then stopped and started shaking.

"All I did was answer the phone. You deserve this Renee, you've been the one who's worked day and night. Do you have everything you need for tomorrow night's opening?" Aunt Sandra continued.

"Yes I do. I found the finishing touches to the entrance today at the market," mom replied.

"Good, remember the car will be there at 6:00 p.m. Is my godchild coming?"

"Hi Aunt Sandra, yes I'll be there. Thank you for my new jeans," I yelled pulling them out and holding them up to me.

"No problem, you're my baby. I'll see ya'll tomorrow evening."

"Can you believe it? I don't know what to say," mom began turning on her old school music and pouring herself a glass of wine to celebrate.

"Come on, let's dance," she said grabbing my hand swirling me around.

"Mom, I'm so proud of you!" I said hugging her. Mom started her business about 10 years ago, and I was happy to finally see things taking off. She hadn't been really active in my life, I mean we always lived fabulous, but she traveled a lot.

Now she's the designer to the stars and she's finally taking some interest in me. It's funny, since I graduated from high school she's tried to put away some of her workaholic ways, but she can't help herself.

We danced for a while, but it was soon over when she grabbed her bags and told me she was going downstairs to her office.

We had to meet the Lyles in the morning and I planned to be there because I needed to make some extra money for the summer. I texted my best friend Tiffany to see if she wanted to go with us.

"U comin n the mornin?"

"No…snooze fest," she replied.

"So…" I responded.

"Just call me when you're done," she texted back.

Shortly after Tiffany's last text, I received my nightly text from Lois, my other best friend. We all went to church together but Lois was the one who always took her walk with God seriously. She prays for everyone and at the end of each day she sends a positive scripture.

I woke up to the door bell ringing twenty times. It was my mother's staff. There was Leslie, my mom's personal assistant, Josh the carpenter, and Jallel, who my mom says has the best eye for color and fabric she's ever seen.

"Come on Brea, we'll be leaving in a few minutes," mom said through the intercom.

4

"I hate that thing," I said to myself as I ran in the bathroom to get dressed. I can't believe I over slept. Good thing I showered and got my clothes ready last night. I picked the closest thing to a business suit I owned and ran downstairs.

By the time I got downstairs, a black SUV had pulled up.

"Renee, the car is here," said Leslie rushing us out the door.

Everyone jumped into the SUV like we were the FBI on our way to solve a case. They listened to wack music and asked me far too many questions.

"Okay, I see you with your little suit on," began Jallel from the front seat.

"Um, um. I'm not worried about that suit, I want to know, who you dating?" began Josh.

"And her cheechees are finally growing," Leslie added. I looked down in despair. It was true, I hadn't dated much, well at all and I was still pretty skinny, but momma told me she didn't start to fill out until after high school.

"I'm getting a little something, something," I said trying to sound convincing looking at myself.

"My friend Tyrese says I have a donk in the making," I continued.

"Lord child, Tyrese lied to you," teased Jallel.

"Ya'll leave my child alone," mom interrupted putting her arm around me.

"She looks just fine," she said pinching my cheeks.

I was so thankful when we finally pulled up to the big beautiful house because I was about to yank out my hair.

A young Latino woman opened the door.

"Good morning, Ms. Boyd, I'm Charlie, Mrs. Lyles personal assistant. Please follow me this way, she's waiting to meet you," she said with a thick Latin accent.

We all stood there for a minute because we didn't know what she said until she signaled for us to follow her.

She led the staff to a huge area which opened up into a massive set of stairs. Mom had decorated some houses, but none ever this big. A beautiful dark skinned woman was standing in the open area waiting for us.

"Renee, good morning, thanks so much for agreeing to decorate our home," she began kissing my mom and shaking everyone's hand. "Darron has a meeting so he won't be able to join us, but he told me he can't wait to see our home after you're done."

"No problem, I'm looking forward to meeting him. In the meantime, I want you to meet my staff. This is Jallel, Leslie and Josh and this is my daughter Brea," mom introduced.

"Nice to meet you all, please sit down, is anyone thirsty?" She continued.

"No we're fine, thank you," my mom replied.

"Brea, right? Would you like to go out by the pool with my son and his friends, they're having a party?" she asked summoning her personal assistant.

"Charlie, will you take Brea to Ms. Pitts please?"

"Great," I thought to myself. "I'm crashing her son's pool party in a church suit."

"Brea, this house is fantastic," she began with her thick Latin accent. "It has 12 bedrooms, 7 bathrooms, 2 Jacuzzis, an indoor and outdoor pool, a waterfall and finally this magnificent 1,000 square foot kitchen. Here we are. Ms. Pitts this is Brea, the designer's daughter. Could you please make her feel welcome?" she asked smiling.

Ms. Pitts just looked at her and smiled while shaking her head in agreement.

"Bueno, nice to meet you Brea. I go now," Charlie said turning around and walking out quickly.

"Child, I don't understand a word that woman says, what's your name again?" She said with a beautiful smile on her face and a heavy Louisiana accent. Ms. Pitts was a big black woman who looked like she didn't play, and she bossed around everyone in the kitchen.

"Brea," I quickly replied.

"Come on baby and have a seat," she welcomed. As I sat on a tall stool, I heard music coming from the swimming pool.

"Are you hungry?" She continued in a nice voice.

"No ma'am," I responded. "But I would like something to drink."

"Of course," she said getting a glass out of the cabinet and filling it with lemonade.

As she poured my drink, I started walking toward the music.

"Go on dear," she encouraged. "Here, take your drink. Craig, the Lyles' son, and a few of his friends are having a pool party. You can go hang out with them if you want," she encouraged.

"Thank you," I said taking the glass and walking toward the patio until the pool came into full view.

Girls were dancing provocatively and the boys were grabbing them and throwing them in the pool.

I party with my friends, but for some reason looking at them made me feel trashy. I turned around to go back into the house when a tall light skinned boy appeared out of nowhere.

"Hey, hey, are you lost?" He said touching my shoulder.

"I'm sorry, yeah I think I am. I'm looking for the pool party. Ms. Pitts sent me out here," I explained slightly pulling my shoulder away.

"I'm sorry ma, I didn't mean to scare you," he said letting my shoulder go and stepping back. "What's your name?"

"Brea Boyd," I responded coldly.

"Oh yeah, you must be Renee Boyd's daughter? I'm Craig, Sydney and Darron Lyles are my parents. My Mom told me ya'll were coming by. Nice to meet you," he continued shaking my hand.

"Excuse them fools, they always got the wrong thing on their mind," he explained stepping in front of the patio door to block the almost naked girls.

"Hey, this is your house. You can do whatever you want. I have to go back to work helping my mom anyway as you can tell by my clothes," I said trying to look professional.

"Oh, excuse me ma'am," he said stepping out of the way.

"Will I see you again?" he continued.

"I don't know, I just help with measurements," I said flippantly opening the door.

"Well, I hope I do see you again, business lady," he said smiling.

"Maybe," I replied almost walking into the door.

After I walked out, I leaned on the wall for a moment to catch my breath. Swoosh, he was fine! Tall, handsome and a body like WOW!

By the time I snapped out of my trance and figured out how to make it back to the front of the house, mom and Mrs. Lyles were finished with their meeting.

Mom wrapped things up pretty quickly after that and I tried to think of anything other than Craig Lyles.

Later that evening, I had to go with my mom to her haughty-taughty restaurant opening. I was her date because she doesn't have much time to meet anyone and I think she's still stuck on my dad.

Just like Aunt Sandra said, the car was there at 6:00 p.m. on the dot.

I wore a short silver dress with my hair swept into a soft bun and bangs. My shoes were "what that was." Mom had been getting ready all day, and she and Aunt Sandra looked old school good.

We pulled up to the restaurant where there were all kinds of expensive cars I'd never seen before with older people getting out. Everyone had on fancy clothes and you could tell they were all rich.

We'd barely entered the restaurant when the owners came out and greeted us. The husband was a short bald headed brother, and the wife was a tall light skinned lady.

"Renee, we love you so much. Thank you for everything you've done for us. The restaurant is beautiful," they both screamed while hugging my mother kissing her on both cheeks.

"Cheryl and Quincy, I'm so happy for you, and I have the final touch I wanted to add," mom said returning their hugs.

"This is my daughter, Brea and of course, you know Sandra Adams, my agent."

"This is Cheryl and Quincy Straight."

She signaled and two men came in holding a beautiful portrait of the owners. I thought they were going to cry. They hung it at the entrance and we spent a little time taking pictures in front of it.

After all the pictures, we walked into the restaurant and my eyes almost rolled on the floor. It was an upscale Italian food restaurant decorated like a beautiful Italian villa with soft colors, and statues.

The doors opened at 7:00 p.m. and a rush of about 100 people came in.

I found a table to sit at while my mother worked the room introducing herself to every player and entertainer she met.

Music was playing softly in the background, so I decided to eat and text. I dropped my napkin on the floor and when I bent over to pick it up, a hand appeared.

"Here you go business lady," said a voice I knew.

"Thank you," I said looking up with a big goofy smile on my face. It was Craig. I wondered if he knew I was going to be here tonight.

"I heard your mom decorated this place. She got some skills," he complimented while pulling out a chair to sit down.

"May I?" he asked pointing at the chair with a smile on his face that made me want to kiss him.

"It's a free country," I responded like I didn't care.

"Yeah, and there are a lot of places to sit in the country, but I want to sit here with you." How could I resist?

"Okay, you can sit down," I said looking at him suspiciously.

"Thank you. Do you want something to drink?"

"No, I'm fine."

"Yes you are," he said slapping his hands together and licking his lips.

"That was so lame," I said laughing.

"Awe, why you want to tease me? I'm just saying you banging."

"Thank you."

"So where do you go to school?" he continued.

"I graduated from Winfro Girls' Academy this year and I won a dance scholarship to go to college. I'm going to Marion Women's University so I can still help my mom with the business."

"That's cool, I graduated from East Point. We used to hang out with some girls from Winfro, but I've never met you before," he said with a big smile on his face.

"Don't smile so big. I'm not like most of the girls from Winfro, I don't sleep with everyone on the football team."

"How you gone put words in my mouth? I didn't say anything," he said grinning.

"Whatever. Where are you going to college?" I continued.

"I haven't made up my mind because there are about 100 colleges after me for my basketball skills," he bragged.

"Um, you play basketball?" I continued with a smirk on my face.

"What's that look? You should come see me play sometime."

"Maybe."

As the night went on, he introduced me to some of his friends and at the end of the evening he walked me and mom to the car.

As soon as he shut the door, mom started in.

"That little boy sure was in your face all night," she began.

Dang, I thought she was networking.

"We're just friends mom," I assured her.

"Okay, because you know his parents are my clients, and I don't want ya'll's drama to mess up my money," she warned.

"Wow, Renee you should be celebrating your huge commission and not complaining about a handsome boy being attracted to your beautiful daughter," Aunt Sandra said winking her eye at me.

"Yeah, mom and I already know, nothing comes between you and your money," I said looking out of the window thinking about the day I spent with Craig.

When we got home, I texted Tiffany.

"Whr r u?"

"@ home...whr r u?" she responded.

"Call me," I texted back.

I picked up the phone on the first ring.

"What's up?" she asked suspiciously.

"Oh, I don't know, just getting back from hanging out with Craig Lyles," I said arrogantly.

"What?" she asked in a confused voice.

"I told you we were going over there this morning," I reminded.

"You told me you were going to do some measurements and color comparisons for your mom. That's boring, so that's why I didn't go, but if I'd known Craig was going to be there, I definitely would've went," she continued.

"So what does that say about our friendship? You'll only hang out with me for fun?" I asked in a pouting voice.

"Girl please, your momma made you go," we both started laughing.

"Tell me everything, what did ya'll do and does he look as good in person as he does in the magazines?"

"Which one, Craig or his dad?" I asked being funny.

"You know who I'm talking about," she said impatiently.

"Okay, okay. Yes, he's even finer in person than he is in the magazines," I confirmed.

"I knew it!" She exclaimed.

"My cousin used to talk to one of his friends and she said he was fine," she continued.

"We met this morning at the house. He was having a pool party with a bunch of boppers barely dressed standing around. I was getting ready to go because I had on a business suit."

"You mean a church suit," Tiffany laughed.

"Business suit, church suit, it doesn't matter because he stopped me."

"Um, um, um," Tiffany said smacking her teeth.

"Then I saw him again at the restaurant opening tonight."

"Oh I wanted to go, but my brother came home from school," she apologized.

"That's alright, you would've been in the way," I teased.

"Forget you. What happens now?" she asked.

"He asked me to go on a date with him," I explained.

"Sounds like ya'll have already been on two dates to me. I know you're feeling him."

"I don't know, I haven't really made up my mind yet," I said trying to sound shy.

"Stop acting like you don't want to go. Say yes," she urged.

"Maybe we can all go to the fair this weekend," she suggested.

"Who are we all? I don't even know him that well yet," I responded.

The phone rang, Craig's name popped up on the caller I.D.

"It's Craig," I said nervously. We both started screaming.

"Say yes, Brea," she sang as we hung up the telephone.

"Hello."

Chapter Two: Almost Doesn't Count

"What's up?" The smooth voice began.

"May I ask who's calling?" I teased.

"Oh, so you a comedian now?"

"Hi Craig."

"Hi Brea. It's not too late for you to talk on the phone is it?" He asked jokingly.

"Who's being funny now?" I replied.

"Did you have a good time tonight?" he asked.

"Yes, it was hilarious seeing all those old people dance."

"Yeah, your momma was getting it," he teased.

"At least my momma can almost dance, your daddy is still doing the moon walk."

"Tragic, I know. I've asked him to stop, but what can you say. Have you thought about what I asked you?" he continued in a more serious voice.

"What, about going out with you?" I confirmed.

"Yeah. I'd like to show you a good time and spoil you," he explained.

"Um, a good time could be nice and I love to be spoiled."

"I promise you, you'll have a great time," he clarified.

"Okay, I replied without a fight." All I was thinking is "wow!" This boy got some go. His voice was so sexy and I could tell I was in for a good time.

"You looked so beautiful tonight. You sure are the wifey type," he continued.

"Craig, you don't even know me. I like taking things slow," I explained.

"That's cool, I respect slow. I'm just the kind of guy who likes to go after what I want."

"Well, I don't know if I like the words, "go after," but I do guess one date is alright," I agreed.

"I know guys are all over you so I feel privileged that you said yes."

"Really? I haven't been seeing anyone lately, well ever," I confessed. I heard him laughing quietly.

"That's surprising. You're so fine I can't believe you've never had a man?"

"I haven't had sex if that's what you mean, but I've talked to boys on the telephone. Have you?" I continued.

"What? Ever talked to boys on the phone?" He asked jokingly.

"You know what I mean, are you a virgin?" I asked suspiciously.

"Naw, not exactly, but you get a little tired of girls always throwing themselves at you. I'm looking for more than just sex," he explained.

"Yeah, yeah," I thought to myself.

"All boys want to get with a virgin," I replied.

"Naw shortey, all guys want to get with the wifey type," he explained.

"Well, let's start with the first date," I concluded.

We went on the first date, and many more after that. Spending time with him felt right. It had already been a month and we were getting closer. He always made me laugh and everywhere we went was first class.

Mom started suspecting something because I'd been spending a lot of time away from home.

I finally decided it was alright for him to meet Tiffany, but I wasn't ready to tell mom.

I'd kept our relationship private until I knew for sure. Even though Tiffany and I talked about him all the time, I decided it was time for her to meet him in person.

We planned to go bowling. Tiffany met me at my house so we could get dressed.

"So Brea, you feeling Craig?" she began laying across my bed taking pictures of herself on her cell phone.

"You just being nosey," I replied snatching the pillow from under her head.

"Don't nobody care about that nappy headed boy," she said changing poses.

"Girl, you better stop taking all those pictures before you get arrested for child porn," I teased.

"Don't try and roast on me, we're here to talk about you and Mr. Long Dollars. Does your mother know yet?" she continued.

"Well, that really depends on what your definition of 'know' is," I said hesitantly.

"Okay, I take that as a no."

"Take it how you want. I'm grown and I can talk to who I want. Why do I have to always clear everything with Renee Boyd?"

"Cause she crazy and she pays your bills. Besides if she finds out you dating one of her client's sons, you already know."

"I already know what?" I asked like I didn't know.

"You remember that time in the 5th grade when she whipped you for beating up Jojo who turned out to be the son of the man who gave her a big break into the business," she teased snapping a picture of me.

"How you gone go back to 5th grade? I like him and I'll let her know when the time is right. Anyway, she's been too busy all my life why she trying to act so concerned now?" I said crossing my arms and flopping on the bed.

"I want to make sure I like him first," I tried to explain.

"Um, okay whatever you say."

As we talked, I got a text from Craig telling me he couldn't wait to see me. I was showing it to Tiffany when my mom busted in my room with no warning.

"Hey ladies, what ya'll doing?" She asked without knocking.

I almost broke my finger trying to erase the message before she saw it.

"Nothing momma, it would've been nice if you'd knocked," I said jumping up.

"Uh oh, well it would've been nice if you'd paid the mortgage this month. Ya'll must be up to something? What's going on Tiffany, where ya'll going?"

"Momma, stop it. We're just hanging out with friends at the bowling alley," I explained.

"Alright, alright, I'm gonna let you make it this time because I've got a meeting. Don't make me…"

"I know, come to the bowling alley and beat me for being fast even though you've never actually beaten me," I smirked.

"You know me too well. Okay have fun and I'll see ya'll at a decent hour."

When we got to the bowling alley, Craig was standing outside talking to his friend, Justin. I picked up Lois, and a few of our other friends met us there.

"Hey baby," Craig said hugging me and kissing my cheek when we got out of the car. Some other guys walked up that I recognized from the restaurant opening.

"These are my homeboys, Tim and Dan and you already know Justin."

I introduced all my friends and we all walked in together. The guys kept elbowing one another. I guess that meant we looked good.

We split the teams into boys and girls and by the end of the game, we were tied. It was my turn to bowl and I knew I could help us win. As I picked up the ball, Craig walked up to me.

"I just wanted to tell you not to be nervous," he said touching my hair.

"Back up, back up!" I said trying to concentrate.

"You're trying to make me mess up," I continued lifting the bowling ball.

"Prepare to be whipped!" I shouted as I released the ball.

It rolled down the lane slowly. It kept rolling straight and knocked down all the pins. I jumped so high, I almost touched the ceiling. I started to dance one of the old school dances I'd seen my mom do.

It was Craig's turn. I walked over to him and kissed him on the cheek.

"Real funny, Brea," he said looking forward.

As he released the ball, it started out fine and then it went to the right. He left three pins standing. All the girls jumped up and down and the guys were mad. As we all put our shoes on, I teased Craig.

"Baby, you mad?" I asked in a sweet voice.

"I let you win," he explained.

"Thank you," I said winking.

Everyone seemed to be having a good time, so we went to the burger spot everyone goes to after the games. Since school was out, we just hung out until the police ran us away.

There were a lot of people from East Point and Winfro there. My girls and I wanted to see how the guys were gonna treat us with all these girls around.

Craig told us to park next to him so we could all sit on the cars. My friends sat on my car and I sat on Craig's car and he leaned back on me between my legs.

"You have fun tonight?" He whispered in my ear leaning back and rubbing my leg.

"Yes," I replied kissing him. There was no denying it. I was feeling Craig and he was definitely feeling me.

I saw Tiffany cutting her eyes at me so I stuck my tongue out at her.

His friend, Dan, pulled out a blunt and another one of his friends pulled out a bottle of something.

"Let's get this night really started," Dan shouted.

Of course Tiffany was the first one pouring her a drink and lighting up the blunt.

"Tiffany," I said pulling her arm. "Girl, people have camera phones and you out here acting. Stop it or I'm leaving now!" I whispered angrily.

"Girl if you don't stop messing up my high. Stop acting brand new," she said pulling away from me.

"Tiffany," exclaimed Lois peering over her glasses.

We both turned around to see Craig taking a hit of the blunt too.

"You smoke?" I asked in disgust.

"Oh baby, come on now. Calm down, we just chillin," he explained. He tried to pass it to me. I looked at him real crazy.

"Don't mind her, I'll take her hit," said Shauntee another one of our friends grabbing the blunt.

Lois was very upset and I could tell she was ready to go home. She kept twisting the cross she wore on her necklace.

"Craig, why did you do that?" I asked.

"Do what?" he asked in a confused voice.

"I don't smoke and I don't like guys who do," I explained with much attitude.

"Brea, if you don't indulge all you have to say is no," interrupted Dan.

"So are you telling me you don't want to go out with me because I smoke a little?" Craig asked sounding a little angry.

"No, I'm saying I don't like it. Why do you have to act like that?"

"Dog Brea, loosen up!" exclaimed his friend Justin handing me a drink.

"I don't drink either," I said knocking the drink to the ground and walking off.

"Hi Craig," said some girl walking up as I stormed off. Even though I was mad, I stopped to see who she was.

"What's up?" said Dan sounding desperate.

"What's up?" Craig said walking by her and following me.

"Brea, calm down baby, I'm sorry, we're just trying to have some fun. Don't just walk away," he begged.

"I'm sorry," he continued kissing me gently on the cheek and on my neck.

"Alright, alright," I said pushing him off me.

"I think we're still learning things about each other. I feel if you want me to be with you, we have to be willing to respect each other. Besides, smoking isn't good for your basketball career," I said whispering.

"Baby, you don't have to worry about my basketball career, just be happy tonight," he said kissing me on my forehead.

I don't know why, but when it comes to Craig, I get weak.

"I'm sorry ya'll," I confessed as we walked back to the cars. I'm just kind of trying to keep my dance scholarship."

"Oh yeah, you dance?" asked his friend Tim.

"I do a little something," I said teasing.

"Naw fool, don't be worried about what my woman is doing," Craig interrupted pulling me closer to him.

"Dude," said Tim in a teasing voice.

About that time, the girl who walked up earlier finally registered in my mind. Tiffany was standing there mean mugging me so I realized I'd better find out who she was and why she was still standing there.

"And you are?" I said extending my hand.

"Hi, I'm Kara, nice to meet you," she said sounding like a valley girl. She was cute. She was tall and had a big curly afro.

"I'm Brea, Craig's girlfriend and these are my girls," I said looking at her with an attitude.

"Girlfriend!" She said in a surprised voice.

"Oh, I wasn't aware that Craig had a girlfriend," she said a little sarcastically looking at Craig.

"I know she's not getting fly," Shauntee replied.

"Well, nice to meet you Brea, I guess I'll be seeing you around," she said looking back and waving.

"Probably not. We don't roll with hoes," Tiffany shouted.

"Wow!" I said grabbing her arm.

I decided not to confront Craig about who she was until we got in private.

We stayed for a little while longer when my telephone rang. It was my mom, so I jumped in my SUV and rolled up all the windows.

"Hi mom, what you doing, checking on me?" I answered out of breath.

"No honey, I told you I trust you. Something's gone wrong with one of my remodels and I have to leave town until tomorrow. Will you be alright here or do you want to come and help?"

"Is that a trick question? You know I'd rather stay here," I continued.

"Alright, you know the rules, and your grandmother will be by in the morning to check on you."

"Mom, is that really necessary? Couldn't I call and tell her I'm alright?"

"Okay, I'll let her know. But you better call her by 10 a.m. or she'll be over here."

"Yes ma'am, see you when you get home."

"Yeah, and I hear that music," she said jokingly.

"Bye mom, I love you," I said hanging up the phone.

I don't know what she said after that cause I was on cloud nine. I jumped out of the truck and grabbed Tiffany's arm.

"My mom just called and she has to go out of town on emergency business. She's leaving me at home by myself until tomorrow."

"What?! Are you serious?" she answered with excitement in her voice.

"Tell Craig and his boys to follow us to your house," she urged.

"Now you already know Momma Lois ain't having that."

"Girl we gone drop her square butt at home on the way, and then we can have some fun," Tiffany explained.

"Tiffany you know my momma gone kill me if she finds out I had boys in the house."

"Well, you'll just have to make sure she doesn't find out," she concluded signaling for the girls to get into the car.

Against my better judgment, I invited Craig over with the rest of his friends. Call me stupid, but I was so excited about spending time alone with him that I didn't think about getting into trouble.

I had them park around the corner and they walked to my house.

"Come in and be quiet," I said grabbing Craig's arm pulling him into the door.

"Dang Brea, your momma must decorate a lot of houses. This house should be on Urban Spots," said Justin.

We listened to music and raided the refrigerator. Before long, Tim, Dan and Justin had gotten into the hot tub, and Tiffany and Shauntee weren't far behind.

"Ya'll coming?" Tiffany asked taking off her pants.

"No thank you Tiffany, my man don't need to see your goodies," I explained.

"My goodies ain't what he's worried about. I have a bathing suite under here," she said walking out to meet the others.

Craig and I went into the game room to play pool while we waited on them to finish doing whatever they were doing.

"Can you shoot pool Brea?" Craig asked while setting up the pool table.

"You'd be surprised what I can do," I said chalking the pool stick.

"Rack 'em'," I shouted like I was a pool shark. He took the first shot but nothing went in.

"It's your turn," he said stepping to the side.

I took the shot and knocked the black ball in. The game was over. Craig started laughing so hard, I thought he was going to bust a blood vessel.

"Stop laughing at me," I screamed.

"I see you bowl better than you play pool," he said trying to hold in his laughter.

"Whatever," I said putting the pool stick on the table.

"Oh come on baby, I'm just playing, don't be so sensitive. Come here and let me teach you," he said handing me the pool stick.

"Who was that girl today? One of your groupies?"

"She wasn't you," he replied putting his hand on mine and leaning almost on top of me as I leaned down into my pool stance.

Though he just completely ignored my question, I didn't push him off, because the truth was it felt good to be that close.

"Is this okay?" he asked.

"Hell, yeah," I thought to myself.

"Yeah, I'm good," I said softly.

Before I knew it, we were kissing and his hands were slowly moving up my shirt. I tried to say no, but my entire body began to melt. It felt so right and he smelled so good.

He gently unbuttoned my shirt. Thank goodness I wore my pretty bra. He pushed me gently onto the pool table until he was laying on top of me, kissing me and touching me all over my body.

I took his shirt off.

"Brea, I want you so bad, let's go upstairs," he begged.

"Okay," I agreed without hesitation.

26

He took my hand and pulled me up slowly. We were still kissing and feeling on each other.

The only thing that stopped us was my cell phone ringing with Lois' gospel music ring tone.

"Craig, wait," I said pulling away still kissing him at the same time.

"My phone," I said grabbing it. It was Lois' nightly text scripture.

"Let it ring," he said continuing to kiss me.

"It's my nightly text from Lois," I explained sending the cell phone to voice message.

"We better stop," I said holding up my hand.

"What happened? I thought we both wanted this?" He asked in a frustrated voice.

"I'm not ready for this yet. I mean I've only known you a few months, and this is a big step," I explained nervously while he was still hugging and kissing me.

"Brea, I only want to make you feel good," he said stepping back.

"You do make me feel good. Too good, but I've only known you a little while and truthfully, it's important for me to wait until I'm married even though I'm not acting like it right now."

"I already told you. You're the wifey type," he tried to explain.

"What does that mean?" Um, he looked so good standing there with his shirt open and his belt unbuckled.

"That means I don't have to look any further. I've found who I want," he explained walking up and gently touching my face.

"What ya'll doing?" said Shaunte coming through the door followed by everyone else.

"Ooh Brea, what you doing? Your hair is all over your head," Tiffany teased.

"Very funny," I said buttoning my shirt and looking into the mirror.

"Ya'll need us to leave so you can finish?" asked Tim with a smile on his face.

"Listen people, there's nothing going on," I announced angrily handing everyone a towel.

"It's time for ya'll to go," I continued.

"Calm down Brea, we cool," said Tim trying to dry off Tiffany's back. She hit him and pulled away.

"Okay baby, we gone roll," Craig agreed buttoning up his shirt and pulling Tim's arm.

I walked him to the door and we hugged and kissed and stared into each other's eyes.

"Brea, I'll wait for you until you're ready. But don't say you're waiting to make love to me because you think I don't want to be with you in the future. You can know for sure that you're my lady," he said kissing me one final time on the forehead and walking down the steps.

As I closed the door, I slid down the wall and crawled into the living room where I laid on the floor.

"Don't be acting sleepy, Ms. Innocent," began Shauntee.

"Um, you up here about to give up the goodies," teased Shauntee.

"I didn't do anything," I tried to explain.

"We should have waited three more minutes," continued Tiffany.

"Well, we know you've already given up yours," I teased back.

"Yeah, but I never claimed to be an innocent virgin. You and Lois always the ones telling us to behave," she continued.

"I know, but everyone has to cut a little loose sometimes," I said standing up dancing.

"A little loose?" Tiffany responded.

"Don't go there Tiffany, I saw you outside rubbing all up on crater face Tim," said Shauntee.

"Girl please, he ain't nothing but a mark. His dumb ass gave me a gift card to Macys. All I let him do is feel me up a little bit," she said waving the Macys card.

"Really Tiffany a Macy's card?" I can't believe you just said that. Tell me you're just joking," I pleaded.

"She ain't playing, she always getting dudes for their money," continued Shauntee.

"Look, I gotta go before my dad sends the blood hounds out for me. You know he got GPS on my car," she continued.

"Aren't you 19?" teased Tiffany.

"Don't be trying to be funny because don't nobody care where you are, Tiffany," Shauntee responded.

"Nobody but your daddy," Tiffany said sarcastically crossing her legs.

"Ignore her girl, she's had a little too much to drink," I tried to explain pushing her to the door.

"Ain't nobody worried about you. You too young to be drinking anyway! Ms. Drinks-A-Lot," teased Shauntee.

"Shut up!" shouted Tiffany throwing her shoe at the door.

It was such an exciting night. I got my phone to see which scripture Lois sent.

"Brea, dnt knw wht ur doin 2nite but God gave me this 4 u: If you walkin n the flesh, you will not fulfill the will of the Spirit."

"Great," I thought to myself.

"Lois and her texts."

Chapter Three: An Unforgettable Dinner

Ever since that night, I decided it was time to tell my mom about Craig and I.

I was so glad to finally get our relationship out in the open. My mom already knew unofficially. Sure she was mad, but she got over it. Who wouldn't? He's Craig Lyles!

He invited us to dinner with his mom and dad. I'd been everywhere to find the perfect dress.

I decided on a black dress with a beautiful lace black blouse over it and red shoes. My hair was lightly curled and hanging on my shoulders.

I wanted to be simple but banging, and I think I accomplished my goal.

Mom thought it wasn't a good idea to get involved with Craig because his parents were her clients.

I have to admit, at first I was unsure, but we have so much in common, and we'd grown so close. I couldn't keep lying about us.

It was muggy and raining when we arrived at the restaurant. I was so excited! My stomach was tight and in knots and my hands were sweating.

My mom was finally going to hang out with Craig and his parents. We were meeting at a fancy restaurant called The

31

LaDeDa. Craig had spared no expense for dinner. He sent a car to pick my mom and me up from the house.

Just as we got to the door of the restaurant, my mom grabbed my arm.

"Brea, you're blushing, pull it together. If I didn't know any better, I'd think you were in love," she observed.

"Mom, you don't have anything to worry about," I said, trying to put her mind at ease. "I'm sorry, I'm just so nervous about him meeting you. I guess I don't want you to embarrass me," I said trying to lighten up the moment.

"You worried about me embarrassing you? You better be worried about your daddy embarrassing you," she said opening the door and entering the restaurant.

"Dad's coming?" I said in horror following her into the restaurant.

"Yep, and it looks like he's already here," she said spotting Dad as soon as we walked in.

"Hey Baby Girl," he began hugging me.

"Hi Dad," I responded still in shock.

"Hello Renee," he said kissing mom on the cheek.

"Kevin," she said grinning while taking off her coat.

"Get a room already," I said rolling my eyes.

"Little girl," snarled my mom.

Even though they'd divorced years ago, mom and dad still loved one another but dad always said mom only had room for one man in her life, Versace.

My dad doesn't come around much because he has a new wife and baby. I think the only reason he's here tonight is because my mother made him come. He moved far away so I never get to see him anymore.

By the time we all took off our coats, I saw Craig walking toward us with a big smile on his face and looking great!

"I hope he doesn't kiss me," I thought to myself. My parents are very protective.

"Good evening," he said shaking my dad's hand, and kissing my mom while handing the coats to a man that appeared out of nowhere.

"Hi Brea," he said kissing me on the cheek. Oh that was so sweet, he's such a gentleman, and my parents haven't punched him out yet.

"Our table is right over here if you're ready to sit down," he said sounding like a Tour Guide.

When we got to the table, his parents were there waiting for us. We greeted one another and the dinner was wonderful!

"So Darron, I heard you're considering a new coaching position," my dad began trying to make small talk after dinner. He's a high school coach and thinks there could be no better job.

"Yeah, I have a few opportunities on the college and professional level. I'll have to weigh my options," his dad responded sounding a little bothered.

"Coaching is a noble job, and with your background you'll be very successful at it," dad encouraged.

"Who says noble," I thought to myself. My dad is so 'Old School.'

The small talk continued throughout dessert. After we finished eating, one of my friends, Todd, who I grew up with stopped at our table. He had a thick green-eyed girl with him.

"Hello," he began walking up.

My mom and I stood up to hug him. We had known each other since the 3rd grade and he was going off to college this year just like me.

"Hi silly," I said as we embraced. "I'd like you to meet my boyfriend Craig, and these are his parents Mr. & Mrs. Lyles," I said proudly.

"How do you do?" he said trying to sound important.

"Who's your friend?" asked my mom.

"This is my girl, Stacey, and Stacey these are the Boyd's and their friends," he introduced.

"So which school did you decide on?" I continued.

"UMC so I can be close to my girl," he said with a big grin on his face. She rolled her eyes.

"Great choice," my dad interrupted.

"Well, we're going to let you get back to your dinner," Todd said holding his girlfriend's hand and waving.

As he walked away, Craig looked at me kind of strange but I really didn't pay any attention to it because the night had gone so well.

"Well my man, I'm gonna call it a night," explained Mr. Lyles. He seemed a bit uptight all night excusing himself to talk on the telephone.

"Yeah Honey, we're going to go too," explained Mom and Dad.

"If you don't mind, I can give Brea a ride home. I'll make sure she gets there safely," explained Craig.

"That'll be fine," Mom agreed giving me that, 'you better behave look.'

We walked them to the door and returned to the table. He ordered each of us a soda and as soon as the waiter left, a look came over his face that drained all the life from his eyes.

"What the hell was that?" he began angrily.

"Excuse me?" I asked in a confused voice almost chocking on my water.

"That dude," he said angrily. I thought he was kidding.

"He's a friend I went to school with. He's going to UMC this year like he told you earlier," I tried to explain.

"My lady don't have friends who are guys," he said with a straight face. I jumped up and grabbed my coat. I was pissed!

"Well, in case you didn't know, I was my own person before I was 'your lady.' I'm leaving, you're being ridiculous," I said grabbing my purse.

He stood up in front of me and grabbed my wrist, it hurt so bad I thought I was going to faint.

"Sit yo ass down!!" He said in a very intimidating voice in my ear.

I fell back into my chair in shock! I pulled my arm away, but he wouldn't let go of my wrist, I leaned forward with tears in my eyes.

"Let my wrist go or I'm going to start screaming!" He let it go and my hand hit me in my nose.

"What's wrong with you?" I said whispering, leaning forward and rubbing my nose! He just ignored me throwing his napkin on the table and walking off.

I sat there looking crazy. "What just happened?" I thought to myself. People were staring at us and I wished I could disappear.

I saw him pay the bill and grab his coat.

"I got a taxi for you. See you when I see you," he said leaving me sitting at the table.

I grabbed my stuff and ran out behind him. The valet was holding the taxi door open but I didn't see Craig anywhere. I jumped into the taxi, pulled out my phone and called Tiffany.

"Hello."

"Girl, Craig did the fool at dinner!" I began excitedly.

"What happened?" Tiffany asked in a concerned voice.

"Todd was in the restaurant with some chicken head," I began.

"Todd Gilroy?"

"Yes, ugly, fat Todd Gilroy. We were at dinner and he stopped at the table to say hello," I explained.

"Where did ya'll have dinner?"

"Tiffany, listen!" I screamed.

"Dog, I can't ask where ya'll ate?"

"He went crazy because Todd said hello," I continued ignoring her question.

"What you mean crazy?"

"He tripped, grabbed my arm and left me at the restaurant."

"What you mean grabbed your arm?"

"Girl, he grabbed me and curse me out."

"No ma'am, what did you do?" she asked excitedly.

"I pulled away and asked him what the hell was wrong with him."

"Yeah right. You don't talk like that Brea.

"Where are you now?"

"I'm in a taxi almost home."

"Where is he?"

"I don't know. He left me at the table, he's so stupid," I complained.

"I thought your parents were there."

"They'd already left. That's it, I'm done with him," I said with tears in my eyes. I was so mad.

"You know men get stupid when they see their girl with another guy."

"Hello, I wasn't with Todd, he said hello to everyone. What would you have done?" I asked.

"I guess say hello and give him a hug," Tiffany admitted.

"Exactly, that's all I'm saying and you sitting up there defending him?" I said angrily.

"No I'm not! I'm just trying to make some sense of what happened. Are you going to tell your mom?"

"No, I'm not going to say anything. I just told her we were dating. It was one incident and I'm sure we'll talk about it," I assured her.

"You're going to talk to him again?" she asked angrily.

"I mean I need to know what happened tonight," I explained.

"It doesn't take talking to him to know what happened. He grabbed you and left you!"

"Well, technically, he didn't leave me. He got me a taxi and he paid for dinner," I said wringing my hands.

"And he grabbed you for fun!" she said sounding irritated.

"First you're defending him, now you're hating," I complained.

"Brea, all I care about is you. You're my friend and I don't want you to get hurt. If you're scared, I don't…"

"Hold on," I interrupted.

"Hello," I said clicking to the other line.

"I'm sorry about tonight," the voice said through tears.

"Hold on," I said clicking back over to Tiffany.

"I'll text you later because I'm in the house now."

"Who's that?"

"I'll call you tomorrow," I said hanging up before she got a chance to say anything else.

"Brea, I'm sorry," Craig began.

"Sorry? Whatever Craig you clowned me in public tonight and I didn't like it. You don't really need to be calling me right now," I warned.

"I'm sorry, I saw that dude in your face, and I felt threatened because he seemed special to you."

"Todd Gilroy? Craig, please, I acknowledged you, your parents and he even had a girl with him," I responded angrily.

"I was stupid, come outside," he asked.

38

"Come outside where?"

"Let's finish our date right."

His offer was interesting. He was always adventurous taking me fishing and skating.

"Where are you?" I said slowly walking to my window.

"I'm right outside."

"Outside my house?" I asked running downstairs to see if he was here. I opened the curtain and there he was with a big brown stuffed bear in his hand and about ten dozen roses laying all around him!

"Baby, I'm sorry," he said touching the screen holding up the presents he'd bought.

"I ain't that easy," I said crossing my arms.

"How do I know you won't put me in that position again?" I explained.

"What can I do to make this up to you? I'll do anything to show you how sorry I am," he begged.

I looked down, because I'd already forgiven him.

"Just don't do it again," I said with a smile on my face.

"I brought you a sprite and I'll leave it right here since I messed up your night cap," he said putting the cup on the porch.

I didn't want a soda, but I thought it was sweet of him to bring it to me.

"And what am I supposed to do with all these flowers?" I asked as he walked back to his car.

"Put them in water," he said climbing into his Range Rover.

As he drove away, my mom pulled up.

"Oh Lord, she's going to see these flowers and this big ole' teddy bear!"

"Brea," she shouted as she came in from the garage.

"Whose stuff is that on the porch?"

"Mom, Craig sent them to thank you for a nice time at dinner," I lied.

"Brea, you don't think that's a little over the top?" she asked angrily marching up the stairs.

"No, I think it's sweet," I responded stupidly. I started to ask her what took her so long to get home.

"Well, you and I don't agree, and you better get that mess up off my porch. I'm going to bed," she said walking up the stairs. She really doesn't like me and Craig dating.

As I climbed in my bed, I thought about how Craig made me feel, both good and bad. Most of all, I was questioning what I did to make him so angry.

Lois' nightly text was about forgiveness, which I took as a sign to forgive him, so I did.

Chapter Four: The Big Game

The summer was flying by and there were only three more weeks left before it was time to leave for school. Craig decided to go to his dad's old college which was about a three hour drive from where we live.

We worked through what happened at the restaurant and since then he's been a perfect gentleman.

He was really excited about the hyp-ist basketball tournament of the year, "The Tri-City Basketball Tournament." Tri-City was one of the biggest events because all the brothers came out to showcase their skills.

Me, Lois, Tiffany and some of our other friends were going to see Dan, Craig and his friend Tim play. To win they had to go 3 rounds of 3 on 3 and then there's the finals.

As we were about to pull up, Craig called.

"Hello."

"Hey baby, are you on your way?" he said in a worried voice.

"Yeah, we're in the car, with Tiffany slow self," I continued peering at Tiffany.

"Tell that boy we're on our way," she replied yelling into the phone.

"You know she's really too ghetto for you to be hanging out with," Craig said in a conceded voice.

"That's mean," I responded.

"What that?"… I put my hand over Tiffany's mouth.

"Bye babe, I'll be there in about five minutes," I said hanging up.

"Ouch!" I said dropping my phone. "You bit me!"

"Don't cover my mouth. What's up with that Brea? He always rushing you, he doesn't want you to hang out with your friends," she continued.

"Don't start!" I warned.

"I'm just saying," she continued angrily. "Lois, don't you notice how he's always trying to keep Brea locked down?"

"Leave me alone. I'm not in it! I'm sitting here minding my own business. Besides, I've never had a boyfriend," Lois said sitting back turning up her IPOD and putting the headphones in her ear.

When we pulled up, the mall parking lot was packed. We had a spot right in front because Shauntee and a few other friends held it for us.

We were setting up our chairs when Brad, an old friend, walked up.

"What's up ma?" he said grabbing my waist from behind.

We all hugged him. He had just returned from basic training and he was home for a couple of weeks.

"So what's it like dodging bullets?" began Tiffany trying to sound concerned.

"I don't actually dodge bullets yet, I'm just getting my orders," he explained.

"Will you be going to war?" asked Lois.

"Maybe, but I was hoping I could spend a little time with you before I did," he said stepping closer to her.

Tiffany looked like she was going to throw up. She'd liked Brad since elementary but he's always liked Lois.

"I heard you military guys like girls with a little more edge," she interrupted stepping between them.

"Excuse her," I said pulling her away.

"I'd like to go, but you have to ask my dad," continued Lois ignoring Tiffany's comment.

"Cool. I'll ask your dad," he agreed.

"Okay, here's my number."

She handed him her business card with a scripture on it.

"Wow!" I laughed.

I waved to Craig to let him know I was here, but he didn't wave back.

The game was about to start. As soon as the referee blew the whistle, it was on.

Craig and his team breezed through each round like it wasn't anything. There was a break before the last game and Craig came over to say hello and drink some water.

"Hey baby," he said walking up throwing his sweaty towel on Tiffany.

"Ugh, you so nasty!" she shouted in disgust.

"You got it dude central up in here," he observed taking a drink looking at me kinda strange.

"You're looking so good out there," I said kissing him changing the subject.

"Already!" he agreed.

It was the final round and Craig's team had to play the winner from last year.

By the time the game tipped off some more of Brad's friends had joined us. We were all cheering and enjoying the game

"Scoot your bones over Brea, let me sit with you," demanded our friend Quincy.

"Skinny?" I shouted.

"You're the one who's skinny. Move around because I'm saving my seat for my man," I explained. I didn't want to give Craig the wrong idea.

The game was tied with less than a minute to go. They passed the ball in, Craig stole it and ran up the court and shot the ball. They won.

Lois and I were so happy, but Tiffany just rolled her eyes.

"Stop hating on my boo," I said closing my chair and pulling out my keys.

"Alright, don't let that knuckle head make me catch a case," she said bumping me with her hip.

"You always catching a case," teased Lois.

"Let me tell Craig to ride around and pick me up at the Fish House." The Fish House was right across the street from the mall.

My plan was to let Tiffany drive my truck back to her house because I'd decided it was time for me and Craig to take our relationship to the next level.

He was celebrating with his friends so I texted him.

"Brea, when are you going to come get your truck?" began Tiffany.

"Craig and I are going to see a movie and then afterwards he's going to drop me at your house," I explained.

"Why can't you just take us home and meet him at the movie?" Lois asked.

"Because this is how we decided to do it. Dang, ya'll need to stop giving me the third degree," I complained.

"Naw, ya'll up to something," Tiffany observed.

"You know God is watching you Brea, you don't want to do something that you'll regret," warned Lois.

"Ya'll, it's not that serious. Is it so wrong for me to want to ride with my man? Here's the keys leave them in our secret place and oh yea, don't wreck my truck Tiffany," I said opening the door.

"Don't wreck your life Brea," Tiffany responded while closing the door and speeding off.

Craig drove up and I jumped in the car. I was nervous because he didn't know I'd made the decision to take the next step in our relationship.

I'd rented a hotel room for the evening and I was ready.

As soon as I got in the car, I could tell something was wrong. Craig wasn't smiling and he didn't seem to be in a good mood. I remembered he looked strange at me and barely spoke to me before and after the game.

"You sure are friendly this evening," he began before I could close the car door.

"And hello to you," I said happily trying to change the mood and kissing him on the cheek. He only stared forward as we drove away.

"Baby, you did so good today. I'm so proud of you," I continued.

"Really? Because I can't tell," he said coldly changing the radio.

"What's wrong Craig?" I asked looking out my window fidgeting in my seat.

"Who was the dude in your face today?" he asked accusingly.

"Who are you talking about? There were a lot of dudes at the game?" I asked turning to face him while searching my mind trying to figure out what he was talking about.

"Oh, so you gone play stupid now? Tim said he saw you hugged up with some dude," he responded angrily.

"Who, Tim? You need to tell Tim to mind his business. That's why he didn't score no points, watching me and what I'm doing," I responded angrily.

"Don't get mad at my peeps cause you got caught doing wrong."

"You're kidding right?" I asked shaking my head.

"So you don't know what he's talking about? You didn't hug nobody today?" he continued sounding scary.

"Craig, I don't know, he could be talking about Brad. If he's talking about Brad, I went to elementary school with him and he just came back from the service. When he walked up, he hugged me and everyone else standing there," I tried to explain.

"So you mean to tell me you supposed to be my lady, and you hugging all up with some military dude?"

"Craig, I'm not getting ready to trip with you about this. I've known that boy since we were in the 3rd grade, it ain't even like that," I said trying not to upset him.

46

"Yeah it's like that. Old boy feel like he can touch all on you, and you, you supposed to be my girl!"

"I am your girl, but you don't have to act like this every time someone says hello to me."

"I wouldn't mind if all you said was hello, but instead you always hugging somebody," he said angrily.

"No, I don't," I said defensively crossing my arms.

"Okay, you saying he hugged you first?" he said turning the radio down.

"I guess, I don't know, why does it matter?"

"It matters because it'll show me if you're really my wifey or just some trick," he said in a harsh voice.

"I aint no trick!" I said screaming. I was completely offended because I couldn't believe he would say something so cruel.

"You're tripping!" I said in a frustrated voice.

"What you mean I'm tripping? You defending old boy? You scared he might get hurt?" he said in a very intimidating voice.

"I'm tripping. Hum! What, is old boy your hero?" he continued growing angrier with each word.

I couldn't understand why he was so upset but I did know he was getting more and more angry and I was scared.

"Craig, please, you're scaring me! Please slow down," I pleaded.

"Naw, we gone find Mr. U.S.A and see who hugged who," he said speeding up the car.

"What?" I screamed.

"Craig, what happened to you loving me and never hurting me?" I said as he continued to pick up speed.

"That was before you were playing me," he said with his lips shaking and holding back tears.

"Playing you? Craig, why would you say that?"

"There he goes," he said pulling up next to Brad's car.

I couldn't believe what he was doing.

"Say partner, can I holla at you?" he said leaning over me and shouting through my window.

"Say what's up man. Hey Brea," he said shaking Craig's hand.

"Yeah, man I was just hollering at you to see if my girl hugged you or if you hugged her first today at the game?" he asked with a cold straight face.

I was so embarrassed I thought I was going to die. I was looking at Brad with desperation in my eyes.

"What?" He said looking at me strange.

"I hugged her and all of her friends," he confirmed.

Craig didn't even say anything, he just backed up and sped off.

"Captain America trying to protect you, huh? I saw how he looked at you!" he shouted.

"You know what Craig, it's time for you to take me home," I said trying to stay calm.

That's when he reached over and punched me in my side, and then he punched me again, and again.

"You don't tell me what to do. You always up in somebody's face."

It was all happening so fast I couldn't believe he was so upset over something so small. I was screaming and trying to hit him back but he was too strong.

"Please Craig, stop it! You're hurting me," I screamed trying to block his punches.

He grabbed my hair.

"You always acting like you run everything and you know so damn much. You need to know how to respect your man."

I was plotting in my mind about how to get away from him while he went on and on about me and my military jump off, punching me each time his anger would arise.

We neared a stop sign across from a well lit restaurant. I thought if I were going to get away, now was my chance. I jumped out of the car and ran as fast as I could toward the people in the parking lot screaming.

I had on a mini skirt and some sandal heels. I took my shoes off and tried my best to get to the people. I know they saw me coming, screaming and waving for help, but they just got in their car and drove off.

By the time I made it to the parking lot, Craig had turned around and beaten me there.

He grabbed my arm so tight I thought he was going to break it.

"Get your ass back in the car," he said shoving me into the passenger side.

"What the hell? You got me out here looking crazy," he began stroking my hair and using a napkin to wipe my face.

"Clean yourself up! Why you make me do that? You know how crazy I get when it comes to you. I'm sorry, I'm so sorry," he said kissing my hand and the side of my head.

"You alright? Come on let's get you home."

"Everything's going to be alright," he said locking his fingers between mine.

I stiffened them as hard as I could, but he just kept kissing them.

I was so afraid and in shock. No guy had ever hit me, especially not with his fist.

He dropped me off at Tiffany's house to get my truck. I didn't ring Tiffany's doorbell because I didn't want her to know how upset I was.

She left my keys under the front mat. I got in and drove off as quickly as I could.

I was praying in my heart and my mind while driving and tears started rolling down my face.

"Hello," I said as the phone interrupted my pity party.

"Hey baby," mom said in a happy voice.

"Hi mom, I'm almost there," I said sniffling.

"Good because I just got back from the store," she responded.

"You sound strange, what's wrong?" she continued in a concerned voice.

"It's just my allergies. I'm good. Why are you going to the store so late?"

"I won't be able…"

"Hello, mom, mom?" I shouted. I could still hear her talking, but she wasn't talking to me.

"I'm sorry baby, Craig walked up behind me and scared me," she said laughing.

50

"What is he doing there?" I asked frantically.

"I don't know, here, talk to him while I open the door."

"Mom," I shouted but she'd already given him the phone.

"Hi Brea, why aren't you home yet?" he asked nicely.

"Because I drove slowly, my side hurts," I responded coldly.

"Okay baby, I'm back, bye Craig. I thought ya'll had a date tonight," Mom continued.

"Is he gone?" I asked.

"Almost. Why? I thought he was your boo," she said teasing.

"Okay, he's gone now," she confirmed.

"Alright, I'm about to pull up."

"Is everything alright?" she asked in a concerned voice.

"Oh yes ma'am, I'm about to pull up now."

She waited to see me park and then she went inside the house.

I debated on whether to tell her what happened between Craig and me, but I decided not to.

As I walked in the door, Craig rode by smiling.

Chapter Five: The Graduation Party

Things had been really tense between Craig and I since the car incident. I've been avoiding him and he'd been basically stalking me. He was texting, sending flowers, buying jewelry, the works. But I was scared, and by now, it was almost time for me to go to school.

I didn't return any of his phone calls so I hadn't spoken to him in about a week.

The last party of the summer was at Margaret McPhearson's house and everyone was going to be there. She danced on the drill team with me, and her dad was some big time bank guy.

My homeboy Quenton, and a couple of his friends went with me, Tiffany and old lady Lois. Her nightly text really helped me deal with Craig and his stupidity.

"The chicken heads are going to be in the house tonight!" Quenton shouted as we drove off in my brand new SUV my mom bought me for graduation.

"Do you have to call girls chicken heads?" began Lois angrily.

"Oops, I'm, sorry Grandma Lois," Quenton teased.

"Yeah, I got your grand ma," she said looking mean.

"Woop, Lois getting crunk," Tiffany teased.

"Whatever," said Quenton ignoring her threat.

"I can't believe we're leaving home! I'm so nervous!" Lois continued.

"Are you kidding me? My parents drive me nuts. I'm excited about leaving and about all the fine college guys that's going to be here tonight," Tiffany continued.

When we walked in, the music was sounding good, and everything was beautiful. They had a champagne sprout spewing out non-alcoholic punch. Margaret was following Billy Johnson around trying to keep him from putting cough syrup in everyone's drink.

I spotted one of Craig's friends named Dan. He had a blunt behind his ear. I don't know what's wrong with that boy.

"Tiffany, look, Dan's here, you think Craig is here too?" I asked hesitantly moving back toward the door.

"Calm down girl, we got our boys with us, and everything is cool. Stop stressing," Tiffany assured me.

"Let's go find Billy," said Marcus, one of our homeboys.

As we walked deeper into the party, I spotted Craig. A cold chill ran down my spine. He was standing on the wall with the same girl from the bowling alley.

"Ain't that Kara?" I asked pulling Tiffany's arm.

"I can't tell and I really don't care and neither should you! Why are you tripping?" she said pulling away.

"You're right, I can't have no boy putting his dirty hands on me," but still, "we haven't even officially broken up," I thought to myself.

"Are you alright Brea?" asked Lois. "We can leave."

"She's alright, aren't you Brea?" Tiffany asked while giving me an evil eye.

"I'm cool, let's just have fun."

We kept it moving, but I made it my business to make eye contact with Craig. He looked at me with those gorgeous brown eyes filled with the same anger that I'd seen before.

I knew it was really time for me to show out. I grabbed Quenton's arm right before he took a sip of Billy's mixed punch and cough syrup mess.

"Come on, let's dance," I said pulling his arm.

"Dang girl, you almost made me spill my drink," he said chugging the drink down and leaving it on the table.

I made sure we stood somewhere Craig could see us. Quenton was really cute and I knew he'd been feeling me since the first grade. I danced all over him and he danced all over me.

As we danced off the floor, Lois grabbed me.

"Oh, here we go," complained Tiffany.

"What was that about?" Lois asked angrily.

"What was what about? I can dance if I want," I said folding my arms while grabbing one of Billy's drinks.

"You know Craig is here and he watched you the whole time, and since when did you start drinking?" she said stepping closer to me.

"Lois, he's here with a girl and you ain't her momma," Tiffany interrupted. "You're too serious, come on Brea, let's move around," she concluded walking away.

The night was fun and I steered clear of "Psych Psych" Craig. The party was coming to a close and everyone was walking back to their cars. They had some security but every teenager knows getting back to the car can be the most fun or the most dangerous part of the night.

As Tiffany and I walked out, we saw a crowd of people gathered around some guys. When we got closer, I saw one guy already laying on the ground.

Lois immediately called 911 because that's just Lois.

As we cleared the crowd and made it to the front, I could see Billy fighting and some other guys fighting too.

We started screaming and running into the middle of the fight along with one fat security guard and one old enough to be my grandfather.

The crowd started running everywhere. Lois ran to Quenton who was just laying there balled up. As I approached Billy, I saw he was fighting Craig.

"Oh my God," I screamed. Somebody hit Billy from behind and he fell to the ground.

"Billy!" I yelled.

Craig looked up at me and started toward me. He was staring straight through me, so I turned around and started running as fast as I could. I was looking at people with desperation in my eyes, but everyone was so drunk and high, I don't think they even saw me.

I made it into the house, but by then Craig had already caught me. He pushed me into the bathroom upstairs.

"You don't see me trying to call you, talk to you?" And then you gone show up with some other dude? Yo, you almost got that kid killed tonight," he began with rage in his voice slamming the door. He was pacing the floor, crying and spitting. I mean he was totally out of control.

"Craig, you were hugged up with some '304' in my face and I'm just supposed to take that? This didn't have anything to do with my friends, why did you pick a fight with them? What's wrong with you?"

"You, that's what's wrong with me! Rubbing all up on other people, you don't think I saw you?" he asked walking up on me with his fist drawn.

"Seriously, I don't know what you're talking about, and if you hit me I'm going to scream so loud," I warned.

"Brea, if I hit you, you won't be able to scream," he said looking at me coldly.

"Craig what do you want from me, what's up for real?" I continued, trying to turn his mind from violence.

"You didn't get my calls, candy, and flowers I sent you?" he continued. "Your momma didn't teach you any manners? Maybe I need to go over there and teach her some," he warned.

"Craig, please calm down! I don't know what you're talking about, but I haven't done anything, and I don't know why you're tripping like this," I begged.

"You here with your ass hanging out and you think I didn't see you dancing all over that dude?" he asked getting angrier walking up on me and putting his hands around my throat.

He started to squeeze my neck as tears were rolling down his face. "Girl, don't you know how much I love you? And you always trying to play me like a fool!"

I was crying too because I thought he was going to kill me.

I was trying to fight back as he pushed me against the sink while squeezing even tighter. I finally got enough strength to scratch him in his eyes and he let go. I kicked him between the legs and opened the door running while trying to catch my breath. I was screaming but no one was in the house, everyone was standing outside. The police were in the front, if I could only get to the stairs.

I got to the end of the hall where there was a door. I felt him on my heels. Just as I opened the door...

56

The next thing I remember is waking up in the hospital with my mother, Tiffany and Aunt Sandra standing over me.

Lois was sitting in the corner looking out of a window praying.

Mom had tears in her eyes and Tiffany looked really worried. Aunt Sandra was the only one with a smile on her face. That goofy smile.

My head was banging, and I was sore and could barely move. I rubbed my head only to find a knot the size of Texas on it.

"So you finally decided to wake up, huh?" Mom asked with a caring smile on her face leaning down to kiss me.

"Where am I?" I asked confused looking at my arm bands.

"You're in the hospital," explained mom.

"What happened?"

"Craig attacked you at Margaret's party," said Tiffany coming closer to the bed looking at me all sad.

"I remember getting into it with him, and he beat up Quenton and Billy. Where are they?" I asked fearfully.

"They're alright. Both of them are at home," confirmed Aunt Sandra.

"No thanks to Craig," said Tiffany.

"At least they're pressing charges," Lois said trying to keep it positive.

"Do you remember anything Brea?" Mom asked in a concerned voice looking at me like she was looking at a monster.

"I remember him flipping out and saying I was with some other guy, and then he just started chocking me," I confided.

"Yeah, and this isn't the first time," admitted Tiffany.

"What?" Mom asked angrily.

"Tiffany, it's not your business to tell. It's mine," I said looking at her with a mean look on my face.

"Well then, you better tell it before she sees it on Youth Tube," she said cutting her eyes at me.

"Brea, how long has this been going on? This boy been beating on you?" Mom asked in a trancelike voice.

"No ma'am. We've gotten into it a few times, but nothing like this has ever happened before," I said innocently.

"Happened! This just didn't happen. He hit you, chocked you and now you laying up here in the hospital," Tiffany said angrily.

"Shut up and give me a mirror," I hissed at her.

"Big old mouth always got something to say. And anyway he didn't hit me, he chocked me so get it right," I continued angrily.

"You sound crazy and don't nobody care about you being mad," she said throwing the mirror on the bed and flopping down in a chair.

Before I could pick it up, my mom took my hand.

"Brea, before you look, I want to know why you didn't tell me?" she demanded.

"Mom, there was nothing to tell. Please let me see my face," I begged.

She let me lift the mirror to my face and I could barely see my eyes. I looked like I was on Star Trek or something.

"OMG!" I screamed and dropped the mirror on the bed. "I can't believe I let him do this to me!" I cried out.

"Oh baby, this isn't your fault. He attacked you. You couldn't have known this was going to happen," explained Aunt Sandra.

"Why you say that, because he's rich, good looking and comes from a supposedly good family?" asked Tiffany in a sarcastic voice.

"Of course for those reasons," mom said turning to face everyone. "But those reasons aren't good enough, I should've seen something," she said bursting into tears.

"Come on Renee, let's go outside for a minute," Aunt Sandra comforted.

"Now how is it that I'm the one laying here in a hospital bed, but she's the one who needs comforting?" I thought to myself.

"You're momma selfish," Tiffany began as soon as they walked out.

"Stop talking about people's momma," demanded Lois.

"Well I'm just saying, she didn't know any of this was going on. The last time ya'll got into it in the car, you were shook to the core and she didn't know anything about that?" Tiffany continued.

I knew I shouldn't have told Tiffany about the car incident, she can't hold water.

"What car incident?" Lois asked in a confused voice.

"It's nothing Lois," I said trying to avoid the question.

"Tiffany, I know okay, mom isn't the most concerned parent in the world. But I should've known Craig was loosing control, and I should've left the party," I said trying to convince myself.

"So you're saying that you have to hide and not enjoy your life?" asked Tiffany.

"No, I'm just saying last night was tense and I didn't make matters any better dancing with Quenton."

"Honey, this is Detective Daniels from the police department coming to take your statement about tonight," said mom interrupting our conversation.

A tall blonde man walked in behind her who had a mustache and a fat stomach. His jacket was wrinkled and it had a big black stain on the front pocket.

Thoughts immediately started running through my mind.

"Oh my God, they want me to snitch on Craig? Tell what happened? Oh no, I feel like I'm gonna throw up," I thought to myself.

"Hello Brea, I'm glad to see you're awake," he began.

"My name is Detective Henry Daniels and I'm here to take your statement about the attack on you tonight," he explained.

"Do you know who did this to you?"

Dog, he doesn't waste time. I turned my head and ran my fingers through my hair.

"Your mother believes that Craig Lyles did this to you. Can you tell me the nature of your relationship?"

"We were seeing each other," I said with a big gulp.

"Were ya'll together tonight?" He continued.

"No, I went to the party with my friends."

"Okay begin there, begin from you and your friends going to the party," he coaxed.

"It was just a party at a friend's house, and everyone started fighting, I really don't remember much after that," I lied.

"Mr. Lyles was gone from the scene before the police arrived and no one is talking, but if you tell me it was him, I can make an arrest."

"I don't know, I'm just not clear on everything right now."

"Some memory loss is normal in an attack like you suffered. I'll give you some time to get your thoughts together, and when you're ready, we can talk," he said turning to my mom handing her his card.

Tiffany started complaining as soon as they walked out of the room.

"Wow, you're here almost comatose and he gives you some more time to rest. On T.V. the officer has to get all the information right away," Tiffany complained

"Well we're not on T.V., but I do agree with Tiffany honey, I think you should give them a statement as soon as you can," agreed Aunt Sandra.

"You seriously can't remember anything?" Tiffany asked suspiciously.

"No I can't. I mean I remember us getting into it, I remember him forcing me in the bathroom, but really after that everything is a blur. I was drinking that stuff Billy had." Oops, did I just say that out loud? Too late now, I was just trying to stop them from asking me questions.

"What stuff?" asked mom, shaking her head like she didn't know who I was, walking back into the room.

"I'm out! I'm gonna get Kevin and his boys to talk to Craig for me," Tiffany said grabbing her purse.

"You're so ghetto. This isn't your problem, and I don't want your goons to pay him a visit!" I said sitting up in the bed.

"I'd be mad too, but revenge is never the answer," agreed Lois.

Lois never wished bad on anyone and this time wasn't any different.

I stayed in the hospital for about a week. I was really there to think things through about what to do next. The physical damage was bad, but not life threatening. My pride was hurt much more.

I didn't want anyone to know that I was being abused by my boyfriend whom I loved so much. On the outside everyone thought our relationship was perfect.

His family sent a lot of flowers, and Aunt Sandra kept saying we were going to get paid and he should've never done that to her goddaughter.

I was just mostly sad. I couldn't believe he had abused me.

Tiffany was coming to pick me up and I knew I was going to hear it all the way home.

She ran into my hospital room with a smug look on her face.

"What?" I asked suspiciously sitting down slowly in a chair.

"It went down today, your momma went over there and confronted Craig's parents," she began excitedly.

"What?"

"Basically she and Aunt Sandra went over to Craig's house and I went along for the ride to make sure Momma Renee was going to be alright," she began like a reporter.

"Or to be nosy," I said.

"Well whichever, I was there. She beat on the door and here comes the little maid talking about they weren't there. Your momma pushed the door open and walked right pass her."

I couldn't believe my ears. My mother pushed Ms. Pitts.

"Then what happened?" I asked in anticipation.

"Your mom stood in the middle of their brand new floor and started calling their names. 'Sydney and Darron Lyles, get down here now!'

"Here they come down the stairs all out of breath. Mr. Lyles got in your momma face talking about, 'You better get out my house!' Your momma pulled out some mace talking about, 'You better get out my face! The maid ran in the room to call the police, I guess, while they had it out," she continued.

"What was Sydney doing?" I was wondering, because I liked Craig's mom even though she comes off a little stuck up, she's always been nice to me.

"She was just standing there in her jewels and some cute shoes," she explained.

"Tiffany, you are so unfocused," I commented.

"Well focus wasn't my problem today. Your momma quit and told them she wasn't going to complete the job.

My mom has never quit a job for me. I felt everything was my fault and ruined because of me.

"Basically your mom told them Craig is going to jail and she was going to sue the pants off of them. It was pretty intense!"

"Did the police come?"

"No, we left after she got her point across."

"Did you talk to the detective again?" she asked quietly.

"No Tiffany and I don't think I will. I'm leaving for school soon and I'm so over it," I said hopefully.

"I'm gone let you make it on that one, I don't want to fight all the way home," she said grabbing my bag and helping me to my feet.

I was glad to be going home, but I wasn't looking forward to the constant pressure my family was going to put on me about pressing charges against Craig. How did I get here?

Chapter Six: Mother Knows Best

"Who's this guy?" mom said as we walked into the house.

"Hi mom," I said putting down my bag. My face had gone down, and all the soreness had left my body but my heart was broken into pieces.

"Hello baby," she said flicking a cigarette in an astray.

"You smoke?" I asked with a confused look on my face.

"Only when she's stressed," answered Aunt Sandra snatching the cigarette out of her hand and putting it out spraying perfume.

"What do we know so far?" mom continued looking in her purse for another cigarette.

"He has a sealed juvenile record, and his last girlfriend won't talk to us because she's too scared," mom said lighting her cigarette looking like a detective.

"Um, what are ya'll doing?" I said turning the laptop around to see what they were looking at grabbing the cigarette out of my mom's hand.

"We're looking up information about Craig and we found out some pretty interesting things about his broke down daddy. I found out that Craig is a maniac in training but his dad has a P.H.D.," said Aunt Sandra.

"I think we can take this to the police station and show Detective Daniels, and with your statement we can put Craig away!" Mom continued.

"I don't want to hear this right now Momma, I just walked in the door," I said walking toward the stairs.

"Oh baby, I'm sorry, I didn't mean to upset you. That's a good idea, go and lay down for a bit and then we can go to the police station. I just thought it was a good idea for us to look up some information on Craig and his family," explained mom.

They were so tacky they didn't even let me get all the way up the stairs before they started talking about me.

"I don't know what's wrong with her," began mom.

"She's in shock Renee. Her behavior is perfectly normal in this situation," explained Aunt Sandra.

"I know and I'm trying to be sensitive to her needs, but this can't wait. We've got to get a full statement to the police before this goes any further," mom argued.

"I agree," Tiffany chimed in.

I didn't care what any of them thought, despite everything, I loved Craig and I didn't want to see him in jail. No, I don't condone what he did to me, but I don't want to ever hurt him like he hurt me.

The morning after I got out of the hospital the house was unusually quiet. I sat by the waterfall in my back yard bracing myself for my mom's constant nagging.

A text came through on my phone just as I sat down.

"Can we meet…? Mrs. Lyles."

"Craig's mom?" I responded.

"Yes. I need to talk to you," she continued.

"Not comfortable," I responded.

"We can talk where ever you want," she responded.

Fear totally gripped me. All kinds of thoughts started running through my mind. Maybe she wants to apologize, or maybe she's trying to set me up. I didn't know what to do, so I called Tiffany.

"Tiffany, Craig's mom just texted me asking to talk."

"What! Are you kidding me? She's probably going to try to pay you off," she decided.

"Tiffany come on now."

"That's what rich people do. They pay people to be quiet."

"Well, I'm not going to say anything," I confessed.

"You're not going to press charges!" she exclaimed.

"Nope, I already told you I'm moving on and I just want…"

The phone clicked, it was Mrs. Lyles.

"Oh my God, she's calling me," I shouted.

"Talk to her," encouraged Tiffany.

"Okay, let me see what she wants."

"Hello Brea," said the voice as soon as I clicked over.

"Mrs. Lyles?" I responded.

"Thank you for taking my call. Brea, I wanted to apologize for what Craig did and also thank you for not pressing charges." I listened in silence.

"Um, I set up a 1 million dollar trust fund for you," she continued.

"Well, that's all I wanted to say," she concluded nervously.

"I don't want your money Mrs. Lyles. Ya'll need to face the truth and get Craig the help he needs," I argued.

"I can understand why you feel that way Brea, but I feel this is the only way we can make up for our son's behavior," she continued.

"You can never make up for what Craig did to me. Besides you shouldn't have to be making excuses for him. As a matter of fact, just tell him to stay away from me!" I shouted hanging up the phone.

I was so nervous and upset, I gathered my things and ran back into the house.

"Brea, what's wrong?" began mom as soon as I ran in the patio door.

"Nothing, I thought a bee was after me," I lied.

"Hurry and close the door so it won't come in," mom pleaded. I sat back on the couch.

"Are you feeling alright? You're acting a little strange."

"Mrs. Lyles just called me," I confessed.

"What! What did she say?" she asked freezing in place.

"She apologized and told me she set up a 1 million dollar trust fund for me," I admitted.

"Really?" mom exclaimed. "She better be ready to get off a lot more than that once we press charges."

"Mom about that, I've decided not to press charges," I admitted.

"What!? Craig could've killed you. I can't believe what you're saying."

"Mom, I'm alright."

"No, you're not. The swelling is not all the way gone and you still have to get a MRI."

"It's my life mom and I'm an adult."

"You're 18 and still on my health insurance. Now I want you to really think about what that fool did to you," she concluded grabbing her keys.

"Where are you going?" I asked nervously.

"Out," she said closing the door.

I jumped up as fast as I could because I was scared she was going to Craig's house to confront Mrs. Lyles.

I raced to his house and crept pass the security guard. Craig taught me how to get into the house without anyone knowing. When I entered from the side door, I could hear Mr. and Mrs. Lyles talking.

"Did you straighten her out?" began Mr. Lyles.

"I called but she's upset and not trying to hear it Darron. It's time for us to admit our son has a problem! He hurt that girl really bad!" she continued to explain.

"My friend at the hospital said she had a few bumps and bruises, but she's going to be alright. I just don't want her to get any bright ideas about spending any more of my money."

"Darron, you're such an asshole," shouted Mrs. Lyles.

"Oh yeah, I must not be too much of one, you still here," he bragged.

"Not for long. You think I don't know about Jackie, Charlie's sister? she asked accusingly.

"Sydney, I don't give a damn about what you think or what you think you know."

"I know you don't Darron. You've abused me physically, emotionally, and financially from the day I met you, so cheating wouldn't be too much of a stretch."

"Oh, so what you saying? Your life is so horrible? I didn't hear you complaining when you was taking trips and buying clothes and jewelry, and all this crap for the house," he said picking up a vase.

"You always think everything is about money, aren't you the least bit concerned your son has seen how you've treated me and now he's walking in your footsteps?" she shouted.

He got up and started walking toward her.

"Don't start with me Darron," she said stepping back.

"Other than that face and that body, what? You'd have nothing without me, so you need to just play the role you were hired for because you looking older every day," he said walking up to her in a threatening manner.

"Yeah, that's obvious, because from what I hear, you been showing up everywhere with her on your arm," she shouted through tears.

"You don't have no say in what I do or who I see. You're just mad because you weren't the woman on my arm."

"Screw you Darron!" she shouted slapping him.

He grabbed her face so hard I was about to call 9-1-1.

"Who are you talking to?" he said as he pushed her to the ground.

"Go ahead Darron and beat me. I don't care! You've controlled me since I was 19 years old but today it stops!"

"What you gonna do?" he said kicking her in the leg then grabbing her off the floor.

"I said what you gonna do?" he said pulling her so close their noses touched. She spit in his face. I knew he was gonna hurt her really bad.

"Please stop fighting!" I shouted coming out of my hiding place. It looked like they both were going to have a heart attack.

"What the hell are you doing in my house?" Mr. Lyles said dropping his wife and turning his rage at me. I ran right by him to help Mrs. Lyles. He grabbed his keys.

"You better be gone before I get back," he warned.

I helped her to a seat. She was crying and holding her side.

"Brea, what are you doing here?" she asked patting her face with the napkin I had given her.

"I thought my mother was here," I explained.

"Your mother? Why would she be here?" she asked in a confused voice.

"No reason," I answered stupidly.

"Are you alright?" I continued.

"No Brea, I'm not," she sobbed.

"I'm sorry Craig hit you and for what you saw. I'm so ashamed," she confessed.

"You don't control them," I tried to explain.

"Yeah I know I don't control them, but I feel all of this is my fault because I knew Craig was an angry child, and his father has always been very abusive toward me. But I didn't tell anyone, and now the sins of the father are definitely upon the son."

"Wow! She's being a bit melodramatic," I thought to myself.

"I've decided you should tell. I'll support you and go to the police station with you," she said straightening her hair and fixing her clothes.

"I told you earlier, I've decided not to press charges," I continued.

"I know that's what you said earlier, but I didn't necessarily agree with you then."

"What happened today is not about me and what I should do Mrs. Lyles," I explained.

"Brea, don't you understand? They're counting on you not to say anything?" she answered in a frustrated voice.

"Mrs. Lyles, I don't want to go to court and tell a bunch of strangers about my personal business," I tried to explain.

"Brea, listen to me. If you don't say anything Darron will continue to get away with this."

"Don't you mean Craig will continue to get away with this? This doesn't involve me, what's going on here started long before me and Craig," I said standing up putting my purse on my shoulder. She started to cry quietly.

"You're right. Please forgive me. Darron has dogged me so long I always thought the money could make up for it. Funny though, I can't find big enough glasses to cover up my lips, or the bruises on my neck from him chocking me."

"So what now?" I asked walking toward the door.

"Now it's my turn. Tomorrow I'm going to the police station and talk to the detective about what's been going on with Darron."

She pulled out a journal from where she was sitting.

"Since I was a kid, I've always kept a journal. In here is everything this man has ever done to me. I'm going to take it to the police station with me. Maybe if you see me step out and protect myself, you'll do the same."

"I can't tell you what to do. I'm not Craig's wife and I hope you don't expect me to go to the police just because you are," I reminded her.

"That's fine. Can I call you when I get back from the police station to talk about what they said?" she asked nervously.

"That would be okay I guess," I answered hesitantly.

"Well, you better get going before El Stupido gets back," she said opening the door.

"What are you going to do? You shouldn't be here when he gets back either."

"Oh honey, I've done this a thousand times with this man. Everything will be alright," she said hugging me really tight.

As I drove away, I felt scared and really sorry for her.

By the time I made it home, mom was back.

"Girl, where have you been?" she shouted as I walked through the door.

"I had to go out for a minute," I responded headed toward my room.

"Brea, I'm sorry about storming out. I didn't mean to dismiss your feelings."

"That's alright mom," I responded nervously. She was still trying to talk to me but I kept walking upstairs. I didn't want to talk anymore.

The next day I hung around the house waiting to hear from Mrs. Lyles. I called her a few times to see what happened at the police station but the phone went straight to voice mail.

Just when I thought something was wrong with my telephone, it rang.

"Brea, turn the T.V. to channel 3," shouted Tiffany.

"And now for Our Top Story," blurted the T.V.

"Brea, turn that down," mom said coming out of the kitchen.

"Hold on mom, please," I begged.

"Our deepest condolences go out to NBA great, Darron Lyles, and his family. His wife of 15 years, Sydney Lyles was found dead. The victim of an apparent suicide."

"Oh my God!" my mom screamed. It felt like I was having an out of body experience.

Tiffany bought me back to reality by pushing the keys on the phone.

"I'm here, I'm here!" I shouted in an irritated voice.

"O...M...GEEE!" shouted Tiffany. "Can you believe that?"

"Let me call you back, I need to talk to mom," I said cutting her off.

"Baby, are you okay?" Mom began looking at me like I'd lost my best friend.

I fell on the couch in complete shock.

"Brea, are you alright?" Mom asked again this time coming even closer.

"I was just with her yesterday," I said with tears rolling down my face.

"What do you mean you were with her?" Mom said in a confused voice.

"Yesterday, I thought you were going over there and I went to Craig's house looking for you," I explained nervously.

"Are you serious?" she gasped.

"Momma please?" I asked lying down.

She ran over to me and sat on the corner of the couch.

"Are you alright?" she asked.

"No, mom I'm not. I saw Mr. Lyles get really crazy with her last night," I confided.

"What do you mean by crazy?"

"He pushed her, kicked her and he choked her but he stopped when I ran out."

"Ran out? They didn't know you were there?" she asked sounding confused.

"No, not until I ran out."

"Brea, how could you put yourself in such danger? I believe Craig and his dad are both crazy, and I found out some things that may support my theory," she said turning around the computer.

"Craig did something when he was young, but his records are sealed, and look," she continued running to pull something out of her bag.

"And everywhere Darron's coached, he's been let go because of his temper."

"Mrs. Lyles admitted he beats her and she also said she was going to report him to the police this morning," I added sitting up looking at the paperwork.

"She told him that?" she said scooting a little closer to me.

"No, that's what she told me," I clarified.

"Suicide my foot, I bet Darron did something to her," she said jumping up.

"Mom, murder is a big stretch from having a bad temper."

"Not if someone is angry enough."

We stayed up most of the day trying to find out more dirt on Mr. Lyles, but there was none. Mom and I decided to go to their house to pay our respects.

I felt strange about going over there after what happened with Craig, but mom was determined to go.

When we were about to leave, someone rang the doorbell.

Mom and I both jumped and looked at the security camera. It was the police.

"What are they doing here?" I whispered.

She shrugged and pushed the intercom.

"Who is it?" she asked.

"Mrs. Boyd hello, this is Detective Daniels from the hospital. I was wondering if I may speak with you and your daughter for a moment?"

"Right now isn't good," mom responded.

"Mrs. Boyd there's been some new developments in the case and we really need to talk to you and your daughter."

"Okay," she responded signaling me to answer the door.

"Thank you for seeing me, hello Brea," he said shaking my hand.

"I'm sorry to disturb you on this beautiful Saturday, but I was wondering had you heard about Mrs. Lyles."

"Yes we have," mom said suspiciously pointing to a seat for him to sit down.

"Would you like some tea or water?" she asked fidgeting in the kitchen.

"Yes, tea is fine thank you."

"Brea, is there anything that you can tell me about Mr. and Mrs. Lyles' relationship?"

"Not really, I only dated Craig a few months and we didn't hang out with his parents very often?" I explained looking at him nervously.

"Brea when we pulled Mrs. Lyles phone records we saw you called her several times today and the text messages ya'll sent yesterday. Can you tell me what she wanted to talk with you about?"

"She told me she set up a 1 million dollar trust fund for me," I explained.

"Did she say why she would do something like that?"

"She said she was trying to make up for what her son did," I continued.

"Can you tell me what her son did?"

I looked at my mom with desperation.

"Brea, where were you last night?" he continued changing the subject.

"Why?" mom interrupted.

"We are just trying to tie all the loose ends together."

"My daughter is not a loose end and she won't be answering any more of your questions," she continued while walking over taking his drink.

"Thank you for seeing me, I don't mean to offend either of you, I know you've been through a lot," he said walking to the door.

"Brea, whenever you're ready to talk," he said tipping his hat.

As soon as he left, mom called Aunt Sandra who called Uncle Michael, her brother because he is the best lawyer in the state. I don't know what they said, but mom told me to keep my mouth shut.

"Come on Brea, let's go pay our respects," mom said grabbing her purse looking nervous.

When we arrived, Charlie answered the door. There were a lot of people there.

Their house looked beautiful and mom's work was still in place. As she talked to people, I snuck away and found Ms. Pitts.

"Hi Ms. Pitts," I said touching her on the shoulder.

"Oh Brea, what a surprise! Thank you for coming," she cried while hugging me.

"How are you holding up?" I asked sitting at the bar.

"Not too well. I loved Mrs. Lyles. Did you know I've been with them since they got married?" she sobbed.

"I'm so sorry Ms. Pitts," I said walking over to comfort her.

"Where's Craig?" I asked looking around.

"He found his mother, so he's had a really hard time. He left for a while because everyone kept coming by and he wanted to be alone," she explained.

"Would you mind if I went up to his room to get something I left here?" I asked.

"Go ahead baby. Just be careful, there's tape everywhere up there. The police have been here all day."

I ran up to Mr. and Mrs. Lyles' room as fast as I could to try and find her journal. Their bedroom was huge, and nothing looked out of place. I looked through her drawers and underneath the bed when I found what looked like the book she had.

I stuffed it in my purse and ran downstairs. By the time I got back to the kitchen, my mom had come to look for me.

"Thanks Ms. Pitts, I couldn't find it."

"I hope to see you again Brea, please call me sometimes," she asked hugging me one last time.

As my mom and I got ready to leave, I spotted Craig standing in a corner. Though we'd been through a lot, I couldn't walk out without telling him how sorry I was about his mom.

That was the first time I'd seen him since I was in the hospital. Even though I hated what he'd done to me, I had to go and speak to him before I left.

"Mom go ahead to the car, I'm going to say hello to Craig," I explained.

"You can't be serious? I'm not leaving you for one moment with that maniac," she protested.

I walked away to say hello before she could say anything else.

"Craig, I'm so sorry," I said hugging him.

I felt my body melt into his and his into mine. He was whimpering.

"Can I do anything for you?" I asked as if I could.

"Will you stay so we can talk?" he said in a whispered voice.

"Craig, I just wanted to offer my condolences," I said pulling away.

"My mom is waiting for me in the car."

When I got in, she was fuming. She was mad because I wanted to say hello to Craig, but I knew how to get her off my back.

"Mom I know you're mad, but I was hoping this might cheer you up," I said pulling out the journal I found.

"What's that?" she asked excitedly.

"Mrs. Lyles' journal," I answered like a reporter.

"Brea, what are you doing with that? I know you have to be breaking several laws," she continued.

"I'll put it back, but there might be something in here that will tell us what happened."

"Go to the last page," mom instructed.

"It's dated two weeks ago."

"Okay start reading there," she continued.

"Craig beat up his girlfriend. It doesn't surprise me, he's exactly like his father. Selfish and mean. Darron pulled my hair and kicked me today because I didn't tell him what he wanted to hear."

"That's all it says," I finished.

I fumbled back through the book but I couldn't find anything that was really recent.

"Is that the journal you saw her with?"

"It looks like it, but she may have another one."

"She didn't say she was in danger, so maybe everything did happen like Darron said," mom observed.

"I don't know Mom, she seemed pretty scared when I left their house," I said stuffing the journal back in my purse.

80

We decided I needed to sneak the journal back into the house as soon as possible and never tell anyone what I saw or heard.

Chapter Seven: There's No Place Like Home

The memorial for Mrs. Lyles was held at their home the Tuesday following her death. It was muggy and raining, but hundreds of people still showed up. Reporters were everywhere and they were taking pictures of anybody they could.

I spotted Detective Daniels who tipped his hat. I smiled nervously and looked away. I felt incredibly burdened with knowing how Mrs. Lyles felt before she died.

Rumors were floating around about what happened but no one knew for sure.

Some lady whom I've never seen before catered to Craig the entire service. I decided to investigate because I didn't know her and Craig looked uncomfortable.

I spotted her at the chilled shrimp table. This is the first funeral I've ever been to but I thought it was kind of weird that they served caviar and had an open bar.

Mrs. Lyles was cremated and Mr. Lyles had her ashes placed in an urn encased in glass and displayed in the middle of the floor. It was sitting on a solid platinum stand like she was an exhibit at a museum.

"That's creepy," Tiffany observed, as I was getting ready to make my move.

"Kinda showy to me," added Lois.

"What?" I asked in an irritated voice.

"That. Mrs. Lyles in the middle of the floor," Tiffany signaled with her head trying not to draw too much attention.

"Who do you think that is?" I asked ignoring her comment and pointing to the female I spotted earlier.

"Why? Are you and Craig at it again? Brea, don't let this memorial make you put your guard down," Tiffany warned sounding disappointed.

"My guard is fine, now do you know her or not?" I asked while crossing my arms angrily.

"Okay, you need to bring that attitude down. I don't know who she is and I can't believe you even care," she said with a big sigh.

"I'm going to find out," I said walking away. I still hadn't told anyone except mom about the journal and I had a feeling there was more to the story than Mrs. Lyles killing herself.

"Excuse me," I said as I slightly bumped into the mystery lady.

"No problem. Hi, I'm Jackie, Charlie's sister," she said extending her hand.

"Hi, I'm Brea," I said shaking it. Charlie's sister? It all made sense. The night Mrs. Lyles died she confronted Mr. Lyles about someone named Jackie.

"Well, thank you for coming to support the family Brea," she said walking away.

"Wooo. Who is she to thank me on behalf of the family?" I thought to myself.

Tiffany walked over to me quickly to see what I found out.

"Well?" she asked leaning close to me looking like a spy.

"Tiffany I swear. You're always so obvious."

"Well?" she repeated.

"Her name is Jackie and she's Charlie's sister," I reported.

"Hum. Charlie's sister? You mean Mrs. Lyles' assistant's sister?" Tiffany clarified.

"I heard Jackie and Mr. Lyles were buddies, if you know what I mean," Lois said like a reporter walking up.

"Oh Lord, we've corrupted Lois!" I teased.

"How did you find that out so fast?" I asked in shock.

"Brea, you're not the only one who can find out things," she said with a big smile on her face.

"Who's obvious now?" teased Tiffany.

"Let's eat!" she continued trying some caviar.

I found myself watching Jackie for the rest of the service because I was shocked she showed her face here so soon after Mrs. Lyles' death. And with all the rumors floating around, I thought she'd be more discrete.

I didn't talk to Craig that evening and I didn't return any of his phone calls either. My mom was still mad but she wasn't saying much and I was glad when I left for school a week later.

Tiffany and I rented an apartment off campus and Lois decided to stay home and attend a local college. She said she and Brad were getting married.

Mom and I'd been kind of cool before I left, but I knew the "Craig Trilogy" wasn't over. We just agreed to disagree.

The first day Tiffany and I moved into our apartment was incredible.

Tiffany's dad and brothers moved us in and taught us some wrestling moves. They also showed us some safety tips and warned us about the spies hidden all around campus who were keeping watch over us.

Tiffany already knew a lot of people because her brother dated a girl who just graduated. After they left, Tiffany and I had a chance to settle in.

"Can you believe it? Finally," she began flopping on a bean bag.

"Our own place! Are you happy?" she said kicking her legs in the air.

"I don't know how I feel," I replied sadly.

I was glad to have my own place, but I found myself worrying all the time even though nothing bad had happened.

"Brea, are you still thinking about Craig?" Tiffany asked walking over to the couch.

"No, I'm more so thinking about his mom and I'm hoping he's going to leave me alone."

"Really Brea, you can't stop being happy because of him. You have to live your life," she said turning on the television.

"Yeah, maybe," I said doubtfully.

Tiffany had already introduced me to a lot of her friends, but I still felt uncomfortable at times. At first, Craig called about twenty times a day.

One day during class, he called me back-to-back so I stepped outside to answer his call.

"What?" I answered in a frustrated voice.

"Why haven't you called me?"

"You can't be serious, I'm in class!"

"It's time for us to talk," he said in a serious voice.

"About what?"

"About us," he continued sounding irritated.

"Okay, here we go again. If you want a chance for us to get back together, you've got to give me some space."

"How long?" I started to say forever because he was getting on my nerves.

"I don't know Craig. I gotta go back to class."

I hung up before he had a chance to say anything else. As the semester went on, he calmed down a bit.

I began to feel a little more at ease and I stopped thinking I saw him everywhere I went. I took my basics, so all my classes were pretty close to one another except for my dance class which was across campus.

After receiving a full scholarship in dance to go to college, I dreamed about using my gift on Broadway.

While getting ready for my first college dance recital, I realized I needed to pick up some of my dance shoes from home.

The only time I had available was the weekend before the event which happened to be the same weekend a big fraternity party was planned on campus. Tiffany wanted me to stay at school and go with her.

"Why do you have to go home this weekend?" she whined helping me load my car.

"It's almost time for my recital and I have to pick up some dance stuff. Besides, I want to see mom and Aunt Sandra," I tried to explain.

"Your momma always down here," she answered in a frustrated voice.

"Are you going to give me a hug or are you going to keep fussing?" I said holding out my arms. She hugged me, sort of.

"I'll be back Sunday night," I continued climbing in the car. I looked back in my rear view mirror as Tiffany stomped back into the apartment with her arms folded.

"Don't be mad!" I shouted out of the window driving off.

By the time I made it home, it was almost dark. As I drove up, I noticed a car outside waiting to pick someone up. When I walked in the house, mom and Aunt Saundra were dressed up getting ready to go somewhere.

"Where ya'll going?" I asked putting down my bags.

"What are you doing here?" Mom asked looking in a mirror fixing her hair.

"I wanted to surprise ya'll."

"Well I'm surprised. Make yourself at home. We'll be back later tonight," she said grabbing her coat and opening the door.

"I'm surprised too," Aunt Sandra said kissing me and following mom.

"Bye Pumpkin," she continued winking and closing the door.

I hung around the house when a text message came in.

"*I'm n twn, r u?*" It was Craig.

I didn't know if I should answer him because things had finally started to calm down, but I needed to put his mother's journal back.

"*Yeah,*" I replied.

"Can I c u?" he continued.

I sat back for a few minutes. I needed to see him but not to be romantic or to get back together. My stomach was churning and my heart was beating fast.

"Is there anyone @ ur hse?" I texted back.

"Yeah," he replied.

"I'll be there in an hour."

I ran upstairs to my closet to see what I had cute to wear. Even though Craig and I'd broken up, he was my first love and I always wanted him to remember what he gave up.

I hadn't planned to stay long since I didn't know where my mom and Aunt Sandra went, so I packed up his things and drove over to his house as quickly as I could.

When I got there, the security guard still remembered me so he waved me right in. As I drove through the gate, I noticed a lot of cars that I didn't recognize.

I'd gathered all the stuff Craig had given me since we started dating as a way to break it off with him permanently. I brought the bear, the clothes, everything. Even though I loved him, I didn't want him to get any ideas.

He opened the door looking amazing. He didn't look as bad as he did at his mother's memorial. He had gained some weight, his hair was cut and his clothes were 'fresh to death.' Even though he looked good, that strange scary look was still in his eyes.

"What's up business lady?" he asked opening the door and hugging me. He took the boxes looking at them strangely.

"What's all this?" he continued.

"I didn't feel right keeping everything you'd given me so I packed it all up and here they are."

"You didn't have to do that, they were gifts," he said sadly.

I felt bad so I tried to change the subject.

"So how's school going?" I said walking past him.

"Way to change the subject. It's cool I guess. We're in football season now, but the basketball team works out everyday," he explained.

That explains why he looks so good.

He didn't even give me a chance to sit down before he started talking about our relationship.

"Brea, this summer I was on some old macho stuff. I've never loved anyone before and I didn't know how to handle my jealousy," he said fidgeting with his hands.

"I know it's no excuse," he continued.

"Craig, you were my first love and I'll always love you, but I can't date you anymore."

"Why can't we put this behind us and start all over again?" he begged.

"Okay. So, how are we going to do that? Are we going to act like you didn't beat the crap out of me? Are you kidding me?" I said putting some distance between us.

"I'm not saying to pretend nothing happened. I'm saying forgive me and let me show you how much I've changed."

We stood there for an awkward moment. I knew what he wanted to hear but I just couldn't tell him.

"You don't have to be scared of me anymore Brea. I'm ready to be the man you need me to be. I promise I'll never hurt you again," he said holding up his hands.

"So what have you done to change? I mean did you take some classes? Are you still paranoid about every boy that comes around?" I asked because I wanted to know what he meant by 'changed.'

"I will if that's what you want."

"Naw, that has to be something you want Craig, I can't tell you what to do with your life."

"Yes you can because I'd do anything to have you back."

I just stood there with a blank look on my face. What am I supposed to do? I was at a loss for words because I didn't want to upset him.

"You seeing someone?" he asked.

"No," I said as if I would tell him if I were.

"Are you?" I continued.

"Yeah, I'm still seeing you or at least I wanna be," he said walking closer.

"Craig, I don't want to talk about this anymore," I said walking to the couch.

"Brea don't tell me you're ready to walk away from what we had?" he asked with sadness in his eyes.

"You walked away when you put your hands on me," I said flopping down.

"Brea, that's cold."

"Craig, you know I can never forget what we had but I want to go slow and be friends first," I explained.

"Friends? What does that mean? You'll call me every now and then?" he asked flippantly.

"No. Slow means respect my boundaries and give me some breathing room," I tried to explain.

"I used to be your air," he said coming closer.

"Well, I can breathe just fine, and either we can be friends or we can be nothing. It's your choice," I said standing up grabbing my purse.

"Dang, where my sweet Brea go? Giving me ultimatums about our relationship? Wow, you look sexy," he said smiling and winking at me.

"I'm serious Craig," I said again.

"Okay, okay. I guess that's better than nothing," he continued sarcastically.

"Don't be that way," I said looking at him innocently.

He clearly wasn't listening to me, so I changed the subject.

"Craig, I'm really sorry about your mom. She was always so nice to me."

"Yeah. People been saying they gone arrest my dad," he said sitting next to me.

"What?" I asked in a surprised voice. I hadn't been home for awhile and I hadn't heard anything other than rumors my mom told me.

"Yeah, the detective said my mom had a large amount of drugs in her system when she died and they think my dad gave it to her because he was having an affair."

"I haven't heard anything in the news," I continued.

"My pops got a lot of bread, the cops can't say nothing until they have enough evidence."

"Where is he now?"

"He had a meeting. He and his friends are in the study. That's why all these people are here?"

"How's he doing?" I continued.

"Coping I guess. You want something to drink?"

"Yeah, you mind if I go to the bathroom?"

"You know where it is," he said pointing up the stairs.

I ran up them as fast I as could to sneak into his mom and dad's room. I couldn't remember exactly where the journal was supposed to be so I put it under their massive bed where I think I found it. I was just glad to get rid of it and then I ran out.

As I was walking down the stairs I saw Jackie, Charlie's sister, walking in the door using a key.

"What's going on here? Why does she have a key?" I thought to myself.

By the time I made it back down the stairs to ask Craig, he'd grabbed his keys.

"Hi Brea," Jackie said in a conceded voice.

"Hello," I said looking at her strange.

"What are you kids up to this evening?" she continued trying to make small talk.

"Don't say anything to her Brea. She's the help," he said angrily turning to me.

"Come on, let's get out of here," he continued walking toward the door.

"What am I doing?" I thought to myself grabbing my purse and following him.

"Sure, but I'll drive myself," I explained.

We went go cart riding. We were laughing having fun and for the first time he seemed like the old Craig. He was calm and at ease, but I knew there was a lot going on in his life.

"So what's up with Jackie?" I asked as he walked me to my truck.

"I don't know. She's been here since my mom died. I don't like her and she's acting like she's running stuff," he said angrily.

"I know Ms. Pitts ain't having it," I continued.

"She fired Ms. Pitts and my dad didn't do anything about it."

Now I felt bad because I never did call her again.

"So is she and your dad living together?"

"She says she's here to help Charlie, but I can't tell."

"What does your dad say?"

"My dad don't say much these days," he said putting his head down.

We stood outside my truck talking for about another hour before I realized it was getting late.

"Well, I better go, my mom will be calling soon," I said getting in my truck.

"Brea thank you for tonight, it really did mean a lot to me."

"Me too Craig," I said hugging him.

"Can I see you again tomorrow or maybe Sunday before you leave?"

I should've said no and closed the door completely on me and him, but instead I said yes.

"Yes, what time?" I responded hesitantly.

"Whenever, I'm just glad you said yes."

"Okay I'll text you when I wake up," I said closing my door.

He watched me drive off and I was confused more than ever. I debated all the way home about telling Tiffany or talking to my mom about what Craig told me about his dad. I decided for right now to keep my mouth shut, just in case he flipped again.

I was watching the latest episode of UrbanGirlz on T.V. when mom and Aunt Sandra finally came in.

"Where ya'll been?" I asked turning on the lamp sitting up on the couch.

"I got my grown card," mom teased putting her purse down.

"To the opera," answered Aunt Sandra.

"Thank you Auntie. I knew ya'll went somewhere boring," I said turning the television off.

"So tell me, Brea, how's school?" Aunt Sandra began kicking off her shoes.

"It's school. I think I'm going to make the dean's list," I confided.

"I have no doubt, you're very smart," she said sitting on our big chair propping her feet on the ottoman.

"She should be, I spent enough money on that private school," mom interrupted.

"Enough of the small talk, what about the boys, are they handsome?" asked Aunt Sandra with a big smile on her face, ignoring my mom.

"Sandra no one says handsome anymore and stop trying to corrupt my future lawyer."

"Mom I'm gonna be a dancer and you don't have to worry because Tiffany already has all the men."

"Lord, it's a wonder that child ain't never been pregnant."

"That's mean mom," I said staring at her with one eyebrow raised.

"Don't mind her, that's one of her better qualities," Aunt Sandra said laughing.

"Have you heard from Craig?" mom continued.

"No," I answered hesitantly. "Well, yeah. I had his stuff delivered to him today." Technically I didn't lie, I just didn't tell her who made the delivery.

"Are you okay with that?" continued Aunt Sandra.

"Yes, I'm fine. I did hear something though." I couldn't help myself, I had to change the subject and get mom off my back.

"Craig's dad is being investigated by the police for possibly drugging Mrs. Lyles."

"Really?" mom said running to sit next to me.

"Tell us everything!" demanded Aunt Sandra sitting up in her chair.

"There's nothing really to tell. All he told me was the police was investigating Craig's father because there was a large amount of drugs in Mrs. Lyles' system."

"I haven't heard anything in the news. When you said 'he told you,' do you mean Craig told you?" she asked suspiciously.

"Momma people talk," I said looking at her matter-of -factly.

"They sure do and they're still talking about what that boy did to you. Please don't tell me you're still seeing him."

"No mom, I'm not seeing him, but I'm 18, in case you forgot, and I make the decisions about who I date. You haven't cared what I did all these years, why do you care so much now?" I said angrily.

I'd never talked to my mom like that and I didn't know what her response would be but frankly, I didn't care. I was mad at her for all the years she stayed out late working and even for all the times she was right here in the house, but I still couldn't talk to her about my unimportant problems. She was too busy making the money she would always say.

"Little girl, who are you talking to? How could you ever doubt my love and commitment to you?"

"I didn't say you don't love me, I said you don't know me," I explained crossing my arms.

"Calm down you two," Aunt Sandra interrupted standing between us.

"Brea, I have to agree with your mom. Craig is bad news and I think you should definitely stay away from him."

"Ya'll are talking about something that hasn't even happened. I'm not going out with him again but even if I do, it's my decision," I said flopping back down on the couch.

"Your decision? Are you kidding me? Not long ago you were lying in the hospital because of him!" Mom reminded.

"And again you remind me. Thanks mom," I said standing up to walk upstairs.

"I'm not done talking to you. This is serious Brea, and you're acting like you don't understand how crucial it is for you to stay away from him."

"Ladies, let's take a time out. It's been a long night, Brea you've been on the road, let's just ring the bell until tomorrow," Aunt Sandra suggested.

I stormed upstairs angry because I felt my mom didn't want to hear me.

I couldn't understand why she insisted on harping on the past and why she wouldn't give me a chance to work this out by myself.

The phone rang as I made it to my room. It was Lois.

Chapter Eight: The Choice

"Hello Lois," I said sounding bothered.

"That's a nice way to answer the telephone," she said in a hurt voice.

"I'm sorry. Me and my mom just got into an argument," I complained.

"Let me guess, over Craig, huh?"

"You already know," I agreed.

"Brea, have you ever asked God to give you the strength to walk away from this relationship?" she continued.

"Lois, I know you're trying to be encouraging but honestly right now prayer is the last thing on my mind and frankly I don't need prayer, Craig is the one with an anger problem," I explained.

"That's understandable, but Brea we all need prayer and right now you need more than usual. You should try praying tonight."

"I guess so," I said with my lips quivering holding back tears.

"I'll pray for you tonight too," she continued.

"You're such a good friend," I admitted.

"Now it's your turn. Tell me, how is operation 'marry Brad' going?" I continued.

"Right on schedule, just like I thought," she confirmed.

98

After we hung up the phone, I cried and prayed. I don't know what was supposed to happen, but when I went to sleep, I didn't have a dreadful sinking feeling and I slept better than I had in a long time.

A text woke me up about 10:00 a.m. in the morning.

"We still on?" It was from Craig.

I laid there holding the phone struggling with what to say.

"Yeah," I texted back.

"Black museum at 3:00 p.m.?"

"Ok," I replied.

I went downstairs to see if the coast was clear when I found a note from my mom. She had a meeting with her sorority sisters. Good, because I didn't feel like answering all her questions.

As I flipped through the channels and ate a bowl of cereal, an ad came on about women being abused. It gave a number to call if you're in an abusive relationship. I thought about calling, but it was only a thought. I wasn't seeing Craig anymore and we were working on being friends so I guess I felt the crisis was over.

I finished eating so I could shop before we met. When I pulled up to the museum, he was already there.

When I got out of my truck, he complimented me and took a picture with his cell phone. He knows I like history so I was excited about touring the museum. The fact there were a lot of people around made me feel at ease and excited about the day.

We had fun trying to name the artists and figure out what the pictures meant.

Being with Craig came so natural. We both still laughed at the same time. How could someone so cruel be so kind?

"Now, why would they make that lady's head so big?" I asked laughing at one of the exhibits.

"That's not a lady," he joked.

We walked around, looking at the exhibits for a little while longer and then we decided to eat dinner at the museum restaurant.

I had to go back to school the next day, but I was enjoying the evening with Craig. As we sat there, I remembered the first time he got stupid with me. It was in a restaurant. I wondered what I was in store for tonight.

"Why does your face look so weird?" he began.

"No reason," I said trying to change my facial expression.

"You're thinking about me putting my hands on you, aren't you?"

"Truthfully? Yes," I admitted.

"Just for tonight, can we forget about what happened in the past?" he asked reaching across the table holding my hand.

"I was under pressure at school, and at home, and I didn't handle it the right way," he explained.

When you're in love, you believe what your heart wants to hear and I believed he was being sincere. I thought about talking to him about going to counseling, but I decided against it. I didn't want to ruin our first evening of peace. I figured as long as I didn't do anything else wrong, maybe we could get back to where we were.

We ended the night with him begging me to take him back. No matter how much he loved me, I knew he had another side and I couldn't take that chance too soon.

We needed to move slowly and it needed to begin with him respecting my boundaries.

"Craig, right now I just can't. I'm still too scared of you."

"Brea, I don't want to hurt you. Why can't you allow me to show you that?" he continued.

"Please Craig, it's too soon. My mother hates your guts, and my dad still wants to beat you up. How can you ask me to ask them to accept you so soon after what you did?" I explained.

"What about you, Brea? I'm not trying to date your mom nor your dad, I want to be with you!"

"Well, Craig, right now I can't do it, and I really feel uncomfortable talking about this like I told you yesterday."

"Alright, I understand," he said dropping his head.

"Don't act like that. Actually, we haven't been a couple for a month," I reminded.

"We'll always be a couple if you ask me," he said looking at me with tears in his eyes.

"Nobody asked," I thought to myself.

"Well, I've got to drive back to school pretty early in the morning," I said uncomfortably trying to cut the conversation short.

"You ready to go, huh? Do you really hate me that much?"

"I don't hate you."

"Can I text or call you?" he asked hesitantly.

"Craig!" I yelled in frustration.

We quickly finished dinner because it felt awkward after our conversation. He walked me to my car without incident.

Driving home I had to pull over for a minute. I felt something heavy come over me. A sadness that I can't explain in words smothered me and without warning tears began to flow from my eyes. Once the tears started flowing, a rush of anger took over and I started screaming and hitting the steering wheel because it hurt so badly.

It felt like my insides were being yanked out. I thought I was having a nervous breakdown?

I tried to pull myself together by fixing my hair but I was devastated.

The phone rang and snapped me back into reality. I straightened my hair and answered trying to sound calm. It was Lois.

"Hello," I said through a cracked voice.

"Hey Brea, what's going on with you? It sounds like you're crying," began Lois.

"I did it, I cut the string," I announced with confidence.

"Are we talking about Craig?" she clarified.

"Who else?"

"I'm so sorry Brea, I know how you feel about him," she comforted.

"I know it hurts right now," she continued.

"Naw it's cool. I know it can't possibly hurt this bad forever," I said with a hopeful attitude.

"You don't have to pretend with me Brea, I know you loved him."

"Tell me Lois. How can you want something so bad for you?"

"Because it's what you want and not what God wants for you."

"Then why even allow me to meet him? I was doing fine without Craig in my life."

"I don't know Brea, maybe God's trying to strengthen your relationship with Him or maybe He's teaching you to trust Him more."

"Right now I don't feel strong at all. I feel like this pain is never going to stop."

"Brea, you're stronger than you think and before you know it, you're going to look up and this will all be over," she continued.

"I hope you're right because I can't take much more." We ended the conversation with her praying for me over the phone.

That night I had a dream that Craig was braiding my hair. I woke up in a cold sweat. He had an evil laugh and it totally creeped me out. I tried to fall back to sleep and just forget about it.

The next morning before I left for school, I apologized to my mom for the fight we had and thanked her for caring about me. She sent me off with some towels and household items which made her happy because she loves to decorate my apartment.

Tiffany was sitting in the living room waiting on me when I walked in the door.

"Hi chickey," she said grabbing my bags.

"You're so silly," I laughed. I was really glad to see her.

"How was your trip?" she began handing me a bowl of popcorn sprinkled with something. Tiffany's a great cook and she's always putting her special touch on everything.

"Uneventful, thank God," I explained.

"How's Craig?" she smirked.

I knew she was going to ask me about Craig because she kept encouraging me to date. She seemed to think the only way for me to get over Craig was to see other guys. She said I didn't like meeting other dudes because I was still stuck on him, so she introduced me to complete strangers and gave random guys my number.

She finally introduced me to a guy named Omar. He was cute, and funny. I walked to class with him sometimes, but I wasn't trying to be his lady.

I wasn't interested in dating anyone for a while. I only had a few more final exams and I needed to concentrate on studying.

"Brea, did you see Craig?" she said again waving her hand in my face.

"Yeah, and he's still begging, but this time I turned him down," I responded holding up my arms to show my muscles.

"I knew you saw his big old head. I'm sorry you had to cut him off," she said hugging me.

"You know I can't stand his ass, but I know you loved him," she continued.

"How was the party?" I asked changing the subject.

"Paid muscles everywhere and Omar was there too. He asked me when you were getting back," she responded.

"Girl, I'm not worried about Omar or any other guy for that matter, I'm trying to get my grades."

"Um hum, whatever," she said as she started to get dinner ready.

I was glad to be back home and looking forward to my dance recital.

Things had been pretty normal the week of the show but Craig kept texting and calling me. I'd answer the phone sometimes, but he was growing increasingly belligerent and angry. He wasn't getting the message about us being friends.

The night of the recital I thought I saw him in the audience. I couldn't even enjoy my family because I kept looking over my shoulder.

My dad gave me some mace and told me to keep it with me at all times. He tried to talk to Mr. Lyles about what happened, but he wouldn't return his phone calls.

I was so glad to see my family and after they left, I met Omar at my truck. For the first time, I really looked at him.

I mean I just looked at him and enjoyed the big smile on his face. I know that I like him because he makes me feel safe and has a great sense of humor. But for the first time, I saw him in a different light. He's an all state line backer and he looks it. Teams are always trying to get him. I'm glad he decided to stay close to home to tighten up his academics.

"You did your thing," he began as he walked up poking me in the stomach. I jumped.

"Dog Brea, that kid got you spooked," he said stepping back holding up his hands.

"Whatever," I said crossing my arms leaning back on the truck.

"I'm just saying, you tense and you never smile," he continued.

I smiled a big sarcastic smile and then I looked down.

"Brea you so pretty, you don't have to look down. I don't know everything that happened between you and Craig, but I'm not him and you don't have to ever be scared around me," he reassured me.

"I know Omar. I'm so sorry. This summer has been rough. I have a stalker," I said holding up my fingers in quotes.

"Well I have a gun," he said spreading his legs and lacing his fingers.

"You're crazy," I laughed.

"Seriously. This cat get out of line, it's on."

"This isn't the wild, wild west. It's not that crucial," I said trying to calm him down.

"Really? Because my sister didn't think it was so crucial, and now her jaw is wired shut. You really need to be more careful," he said stepping closer touching my hair.

A reflection behind him caught my eye. I looked up and it looked like Craig. I must have looked like I was going to pass out because Omar turned around to see what was going on.

"What's wrong Brea?"

"I saw Craig," I cried.

He pushed me behind the car and started trying to see if he could find him. He walked right over to the car I thought he was sitting in, but no one was there.

"I don't see anything," he explained walking back.

"I know he's there," I continued in fear.

"Brea, no one's there," he said hugging me trying to calm me down.

I let him follow me home and he insisted on coming in my apartment and checking each room. Since Tiffany wasn't home yet, he demanded to stay until she got there.

While he watched sports, I asked him to excuse me while I went to the bathroom. I really went in my bedroom to call Craig. I was so nervous about tonight, I had to see if it was him. He picked up the phone on the first ring like he was expecting my call.

"Hey, were you at my recital tonight?" I began without saying hello.

"Yeah, I was there. I didn't think you noticed with old boy all in your face," he admitted angrily.

"Why didn't you call me and let me know you were coming?" I continued ignoring his comment.

"I tried but you won't pick up any of my calls. I just sat there and watched so I wouldn't distract you," he explained in a frustrated voice.

"Well, thanks but next time you need to let me know. You could've texted me or something."

"For what? For you to say no again? I just showed up and now you don't have a chance to reject me."

"I don't care if you think I'm going to say no, you shouldn't be lurking around and scaring me like you do," I demanded.

"Why? That muscle head you were with tonight can't protect you? You lied Brea, you said you were going to give me another chance."

"No I didn't! I said I needed space."

"Dude wasn't giving you space."

"That guy is my friend and he doesn't have anything to do with us," I tried to explain.

"Okay, whatever you say sexy." I slammed the phone down and ran back in the living room with Omar.

The way he said it scared me and I was more nervous than ever.

Over the next couple of weeks, I heard Craig's dad was arrested for killing his wife and Craig hurt himself playing basketball.

All the changes in his life nerved me up. I found myself always checking my phone, and peeking around corners to make sure he wasn't there. It was getting to me. I started having some stomach problems, and my concentration was off. Most of all, I was scared because it felt like Craig had nothing to loose and he blamed me for all of his bad luck.

Chapter Nine: Savoy Street

My mom was in the dark about Craig's continued threat to me, but Tiffany was watching me like a hawk and Lois was texting me everyday about God's protection.

Tiffany knew everybody on campus so she was becoming the social planner for the school. Her next big idea was the end of the semester freshman party and she was really excited.

One evening, I was on my way to one of her planning meetings when Lois called.

"Hey girl, just calling to check on you and to tell you something," she began in a strange voice.

"Lois, are you alright? Usually I'm the one calling you with a problem, please don't tell me you're pregnant," I teased.

"Now you know that's not it, in fact, it's something good." She paused for a second and took a deep breath.

"Me and Brad eloped!" she screamed with great pride.

"Hello, hello, is this Lois 'Ms. I Don't Ever Do Anything Bad,' Green eloping? Your mom is going to have a…Hello, hello." My phone went dead.

My college, Marion Women's University is in a small town and everything is connected by one long curvy road called Savoy Street but everyone called it the 'S.'

On a certain part of the 'S' there's a lot of trees and I always lost my cell phone signal there. I turned up my radio and kept trying to get my phone to work.

I noticed some lights behind me. It was dark and I was driving slow and trying to be careful, so I stuck my hand out of the window and signaled for the SUV to go around.

I couldn't tell who it was because it was dark and the windows were tinted. I kept signaling for the driver to go around but he wouldn't.

He just kept getting closer to the back of my truck. I got scared and started calling 911 on my cell phone. Nothing.

As I punched numbers desperately, he sped up, so I did too.

I was weaving through the 'S' faster than I'd ever done before when the truck started bumping the back of me.

I was screaming and crying. As we rounded one of the more curved sections of the road, he bumped me one last time and I ran into the railing skidding to a stop.

He slammed on his breaks and started backing up slowly. I tried to start my car but I dropped my keys on the floor. When I looked back up, the truck was right next to me.

I pulled out the mace my father had given me and waited for what was coming next. As I sat there whimpering, a car drove pass. I started honking the horn and the SUV that was following me sped off. My phone rang and scared me even more.

"Girl where are you? We're getting ready to start," demanded Tiffany.

"Somebody just tried to run me off the road," I screamed.

"Are you hurt?"

"No, I don't think so, I'm just scared," I explained.

"Where are you?"

"I'm on the 'S' about ten minutes away." While I waited, I called the police and texted Lois to let her know what was going on.

Tiffany pulled up in a truck with about five goons and they all looked scary. Omar came too, looking like a policeman.

When they got there, Tiffany tried to tell them about Craig but I wouldn't let her because I didn't know if it was him for sure. We lived in a small country hick town, it could've been anyone.

She also tried to get me to call my mom, but I wouldn't do that either. I knew she would worry or try and make me move back home.

From that night on, I stayed home during the evenings. We only had one more week until the end of the semester and I was sure things were going to be alright.

I tried to call Craig a few times to make sure he wasn't stalking me but he wouldn't answer the phone. I wondered why he didn't pick up, but I had a lot of studying to do, and Tiffany and I were being careful.

She told her football friends to watch out for us from now on and Omar made sure to walk me to and from class everyday.

I didn't want to think Craig would scare me just because I didn't want to get back together. I knew things were coming apart in his life and I had a dreadful feeling in my stomach.

I felt locked up and I didn't know exactly what I was waiting for. I thought about dying or him hurting my mom, but I kept praying and I tried my best to stay safe.

His father was on trial for his mother's murder and my mom called me everyday with an update.

I was on the phone with Omar while I was waiting on Tiffany to get home one evening when the phone clicked. It was my mother.

"Hey baby, how are you?" she began in a concerned voice.

"Ready to come home," I admitted.

"What's going on, are your studies getting to you?"

"Yes ma'am, I guess so."

I wanted to tell her what happened, but I knew she would worry.

"Brea, are you keeping something from me? Is that fool still bothering you?"

"No ma'am, I met a new guy named Omar and he's really sweet."

"Really, do tell," mom continued jokingly.

"Mom don't tease me."

"I'm not. I'm just glad to hear you mention someone else's name besides Craig.

"Yeah, I think it's about time," I continued.

"I agree, which brings me to the reason for my call. I have an update on, Darron's, trial."

Oh great, just what I wanted to hear, something else about Craig and his family.

"What's going on now?" I asked.

"They put Jackie on the stand today. Honey she should've been a prostitute because Darron paid her like she was one."

"What?"

"Let's see, he bought her a car, a house and he paid for her to get her medical billing certificate."

"Too funny," I said busting out laughing.

"Was he married at the time?"

"This woman has been in his life every since Sydney hired Charlie," mom confirmed.

"How awful," I thought. Not only did he beat his wife, but he was cheating on her too.

"That's scandalous," I said in disgust.

"Sure is. They got his old broke down tail cornered now though and Charlie got charged with conspiracy," she cheered.

I confided I had seen Jackie at their house using a key, but mom told me to keep my mouth shut.

We talked a little while longer about Aunt Sandra, my grandparents and my dad before I started feeling sleepy.

"Well, I'm waiting on Tiffany to get back from her meeting," I explained.

"I get the hint. I'll let you go. Try not to worry baby, the semester is almost over."

I fell asleep on the couch while waiting. Tiffany woke me up jiggling the key in the door and turning on the lights.

At the same time, Lois' nightly text came through and scared me because my phone was on vibrate.

"Wake up," Tiffany said as she busted in.

"Who left these dead ass flowers at the door?" she asked throwing them at me as I sat up.

"What are you talking about?" I asked looking at them strangely as they fell to the floor while I responded to Lois' text.

"Here's the card," Tiffany said sitting next to me.

I grabbed it and ripped it open.

"What it say?" she asked anxiously.

"Drive Safely!" I read in shock.

"O...M....G...! Do you think Craig sent these?" I asked in terror.

"Brea, who else would do something so crazy? You know that fool don't have no sense and now he knows where we live. You should report this to the police," she demanded.

"I'm gone call my daddy. He knows lots of cops," she continued jumping up to get her purse.

I'd never seen Tiffany this upset before. She dialed her dad's number and he answered right away.

"Daddy, Brea has a stalker and he left dead roses at the door," she began pulling a gun out of her purse.

"Tiffany," I gasped in shock.

"Yes sir, okay, okay," she continued ignoring me.

She grabbed a pen and wrote down a phone number.

"Yes sir, we're going to call him tonight. Hold on. He wants to talk to you," she said passing me the phone sticking out her lips looking ghetto.

I grabbed the phone and rolled my eyes at her as hard as I could.

"Hi Uncle Edward."

"Brea, this situation is already out of control. You need to alert your family and report this to the police," he began in his deep judge voice.

Uncle Edward is a judge and he practically raised me, so I had to do exactly what he told me to do.

"I feel really stupid talking to you about this," I responded in embarrassment.

"Brea you're like my own, I love you and I don't care what has happened, I want to fix it. Talk to the police and you girls stay safe."

"Thank you Your Honor and I love you too," I said handing the phone back to Tiffany.

"Bye daddy."

"Here Brea, this is the number he gave me. It's time to call the police."

"I just don't know for sure," I said again hesitantly reaching for the number.

"Girl, it's time for you to admit it. All the little stuff that's been happening around here has to be him. The hang up calls, the truck following you."

"I can't prove it though," I said getting up to look out of the blinds and making sure the windows were locked.

"Look at you! I refuse to live like this Brea. We have to call the police," she demanded again.

We sat down and dialed the number Tiffany's father had given her, and while we waited we made sure everything was locked.

"Where you get a gun Tiffany?" I asked checking my mace.

"Brea, I have five brothers and a dad who's a judge, I've been shooting guns since I was a little kid," she continued showing me an official looking paper.

"Do you carry it everywhere?"

"No, I only keep it here, but if I wanted to this paper says I could. You need to take a class with me," she said pointing the gun like a police woman.

"I really worry about you Tiffany," I said running into the kitchen.

"Don't worry about me. What you need to do is worry about protecting yourself."

"Come on Brea and take a class with me," she said putting the gun away.

"Oh no, the last time we took that cooking class we were escorted out." We both started laughing when the knock came at the door.

This detective looked just as dorkey as Detective Daniels except he looked meaner. He actually made us feel pretty safe though. For the first time, I made it official. I put Craig's harassment and threats on paper. I'd saved all the threatening texts he sent me, which ended up being over 200 for the past two weeks.

I also gave the detective Craig's address and telephone number.

After he left, we put a chair against the door and Tiffany invited me to sleep in her room. I accepted because she had the gun.

Right before I fell asleep, I took one last step that I should have taken a long time ago. I called my mom and told her the truth about what Craig had been doing.

"Hello, Brea what's wrong?" she answered nervously.

"Hi mom, I know we've already talked tonight, but I need to talk to you again about something else," I explained.

"Baby, you don't have to apologize for calling me, I'm your mom."

I told her everything even about the incident in the car. I thought she was going to be angry, but instead she prayed for me. She also offered to come live with me and Tiffany until the end of the semester, which I quickly declined.

Mom told me she'd have her lawyer call Detective Daniels and tell him everything we'd found out. She told me they also found Mrs. Lyles' other journal and it had all the information they needed. The night me and Mrs. Lyles talked, Mr. Lyles came into the bathroom while she was taking a bubble bath and told her he knew she planned to go to the police. Apparently, Mr. Lyles had bugged the house.

As she got out of the tub after she finished writing in her journal one last time, that's when the police think he killed her.

"Where was the journal?"

"Ms. Pitts had it, and turned it in to the police." It was good to know Mr. Lyles got exactly what he deserved.

She suggested we go on vacation after my last final exam. I agreed and we promised to communicate more and not keep secrets from one another.

We waited and after a few days the detective called back to let us know he couldn't make an arrest because he couldn't prove it was Craig on the 'S.'

He suggested I hang cameras around the apartment and take pictures of license plates if I see a strange car. I also put a restraining order on Craig because of the texts he sent me.

It was time for my finals so I tried to concentrate and not think about Craig or what was going on. My goal was to be on the dean's list so my mom would pay for me and my friends to go on the UrbanGirlz Teen Cruise.

My final class arrived and I'd managed to stay clear of Craig. I was so excited because I felt I reached my academic goals. I laid my pen down after the last question on my final exam, and I knew I'd Aced it.

I was looking forward to some time away with my mom and friends. As the professor graded the tests, I messed with my GPhone and programmed in some new songs for the road. I was going to meet Mom and Aunt Sandra at our time share at the lake close to our house.

My cell phone died just as I downloaded the last song. "I'll charge it in the car," I thought to myself.

Tiffany was going home for a little while but afterwards she was coming to hang out with us.

Lois finally worked up enough courage to tell her family she and Brad were married and they decided to break the news during the holidays.

After getting everything downloaded, class was over. All my girls walked out together, but I had to stay behind and ask my professor some questions.

"You coming?" Tiffany turned and asked with concern in her voice.

"Girl, you know I've got to get my grades right, I need to talk to Dr. Lewis."

"Do we need to wait?"

"No, Omar is supposed to walk me to my car," I explained with a smile on my face.

"Well, excuse me," she teased.

"I'm going to the apartment so be careful," she warned patting her purse.

I shook my head. As my professor explained her grading curve, a weird feeling came over me, so I glanced up while tying up my book bag. What I saw terrified me.

"Goodness Brea, what's wrong with you? You look like you just saw a ghost," asked my professor with concern in her voice looking out of the door.

"Oh my God, I thought I saw my ex-boyfriend," I said falling back into a desk.

Dr. Lewis ran outside the classroom to see if she saw anything.

"Brea, I don't see anyone out here," she said walking back into the classroom.

"Don't worry about it, I'm just tired," I said stumbling over my words.

In truth, I knew I saw Craig standing outside the classroom door. I haven't answered any of his calls, and I've been trying to cut him off, and now he's here. So much for the restraining order.

I gathered my things and headed for the door. I thought if I could just get to the open field, I could run to my car.

"Dr. Lewis, I've got to go. You've been a great professor," I said abruptly and ran out of the classroom.

I tried to call Omar, but my phone was dead.

As I slowly walked out into the hall, I looked both ways, but I didn't see anyone.

I felt a little silly and thought maybe my mind was playing tricks on me but with everything that had been going on, I'd rather be safe than sorry.

The police officer told me to stay with a group, but I guess it was too late now. I felt so dumb.

I knew Craig expected me to go down the elevator so I decided to take the stairs.

I went through the first door I came to. I had to go down 12 flights of steps, but I didn't care, as long as Craig didn't know which way I went. All kinds of thoughts started running through my head like him catching me at my car, but I felt at least outside maybe someone would see him messing with me.

I was running down the stairs as fast as I could when I heard the door of the stair well open. I stood there silently for a moment until I heard foot steps.

"Who is that?" I said looking up trying to see who it was. No response.

I thought it could be Omar. He told me he might be able to walk me to my car after my last class, but whoever it was didn't answer.

I ran even faster. I made it to the door and swung it open running right into Craig's chest. My momentum knocked me back into the stair well.

"Hey baby," he began with an ice cold voice slamming the door. I didn't know what to do.

"Oh, hey Craig, what you doing here?" I responded standing to my feet dusting myself off. I decided to stay calm and try to get out of here alive.

"I wanted to give you a ride to your family trip," he said suspiciously.

I was stunned. How could he think I'd go anywhere with him?

"What are you talking about? How did you even find out about my vacation anyway?" I said trying to walk past him quickly.

He grabbed my arm.

120

"You posted it on MyBook," he said coldly.

"Well don't you think you should have called first?" I asked angrily.

"You don't want to know what I think," he responded.

"Why are you grabbing up on me Craig, let me go," I said jerking away. I was terrified.

"Baby you don't have to be scared of me," he explained. Funny he should say that because I'd never been more scared in my life.

"We need to talk, so I'm going to drive you to your vacation."

"Craig I don't feel safe with you right now, and I want you to let go of my arm!" I said jerking away harder trying to reach in my purse for my mace.

He grabbed my hand and tore my purse off my shoulder. Everything fell on the floor. He pushed me up against the wall.

"All I'm trying to do is talk to you. Why you put a restraining order on me Brea?"

"Because Craig, maybe, I don't know, you scare me," I explained as he stepped back a little bit.

"I already told you I wasn't going to hurt you, but you keep playing games. Come on let's go," he continued picking up my purse.

"Oh is this what you're trying to get? You trying to mace me?" he asked pulling out the mace.

"Where is Omar?" I asked myself.

He put the mace in his pocket and pulled me out of the building.

"Let me go Craig, I don't want to go with you," I screamed struggling with him.

He started dragging me but I kept on scratching and biting him.

I guess I bit him a little too hard because he turned around and punched me in the stomach. I fell to my knees gasping for air.

"Brea, I'm gone beat your ass out here so bad if you don't get up and come on!" he said bending down and whispering in my ear. I'd parked my car in the back of the building close to the door thinking it would be safer, now I wished I'd parked in the front.

The campus was like a ghost town, and I didn't see anyone else in the parking lot.

As we struggled, suddenly Dr. Lewis came out of the back door.

"Don't get this old lady killed out here today Brea," he warned as Dr. Lewis jogged toward us.

Dr. Lewis was a chunky older lady with an afro. She moved pretty fast and she looked like she might have fought a few men in her lifetime. I didn't want him to hurt her, but I was glad to see her.

"Brea, are you okay, is everything alright?" she said waving her hand.

"Yes," I said with terror in my eyes because I didn't want him to hurt her.

"I'm sorry, we scared you, we're just joking around. This is my friend Craig Lyles," I introduced.

She looked at him suspiciously and he tried to smile like nothing was wrong.

"Are you sure you're alright Brea because that didn't look like playing," she continued taking out a whistle and some mace.

"Oh yes ma'am, don't worry about us," I tried to reassure her.

"Little boy, this young lady looks scared," she continued reaching out for my hand.

"Who are you? She alright," Craig said walking in front of me.

"I said she looks scared. Come on Brea, you can leave with me," she continued to encourage holding up her own can of mace.

"Naw, she leaving with me," he said hitting her so fast and hard she fell like a sack of potatoes with the mace still in her hand.

"Oh my God Craig, she's an old lady! I can't believe you just hit her," I started to run but he grabbed my shirt.

"Brea, don't. I'll kill you and her out here. Now let's go!"

As soon as we got out of view, he grabbed my other arm and put something over my face. I must have passed out because the next time I woke up I was in the back seat of his truck completely tied up.

"Why didn't I use my mace?" I thought to myself laying there unsure of what was going to happen next.

Chapter Ten: I'm Free

When I woke up, Craig was eating a snickers bar and changing radio stations.

"Craig," I screamed.

"Hey baby, you woke? Your phone's been ringing. I charged it up for you. Tiffany's worried about you," he reported.

"Where's Dr. Lewis? You better not have hurt her," I continued looking around.

"Ain't nobody worried about that old lady."

"Where's Dr. Lewis? And where are you taking me?"

"You got a text from some dude named Omar. He won't be able to meet you after class." He paused and looked into the mirror with a mean look on his face.

"See that's what I'm talking about. I thought you said you weren't seeing anyone, Brea," he said in a really scary voice.

"Craig, what are talking about? You can't just kidnap me it's against the law!" I screamed trying to kick and get loose.

"Don't make me come back there. You gone put a restraining order on me but this cat walking you to class. Oh hell no, I aint' having it," he shouted slapping me in the mouth so hard my ears started ringing.

"Now sit back and shut up. I told you we need to talk."

I fell on my back with tears streaming from my eyes.

"Where are you taking me Craig?" I said with blood coming from my mouth.

"To your mother for your vacation," he explained.

"Oh yeah, your momma called and said your Aunt Sandra will be here tomorrow evening."

We rode what seemed like forever but the lake house was actually only a couple hours away from my school. I felt the car slowing down.

"Here we are. Look's like mom beat us here."

"Craig, please don't do this, I'll do anything you want."

"It's too late now Brea. I've been trying to be nice to you, but you won't return my calls. Stop begging because it won't work," he said pulling up slowly and turning the head lights off.

"Let's go see your nosey ass momma. Her poking around in my daddy's business got him into a lot of trouble," he said grabbing me out of the back seat. I was crying and terrified.

"Is that what this about?" I asked struggling with him.

"Naw it's about you messing with that buster. You've been lying to me. You gone tell me no, but this fool been at your house every night late! You think I'm gone just let that go, Brea you know me better than that. Where your boy at now? Oh let me answer that for you, he ain't here!" he teased.

"Now shut up and come on!" he said pulling me toward the door.

"Now listen Brea, I don't want to hurt you, but I'll have to if you try and warn your mother. We gone go in here and act like we got some sense," he said standing behind me pushing me forward.

"Man this is pretty, I bet your momma freaked this place out with her skills," he said continuing to push me.

He knocked and mom looked through the curtain. As she opened the door, Craig kicked it in and knocked her back.

"Momma run!" I screamed as he started after her.

She stumbled over a bag and then he tasered her.

She started shaking on the floor.

I was screaming and trying to get loose, but I couldn't. He was in a rage. Mumbling and kicking stuff. He closed all the blinds and then he tied me and mom up to chairs in the middle of the floor.

The whole time he was walking back and forth talking about how much me and my mom ruined his life. Then he would stop and started talking nicely.

"My two favorite girls," he said pouring us a glass of wine as mom began to come to.

"I know you're too young to drink Brea, but since tonight is a special night, I didn't think your mom would mind. Would you mind, Renee?" he asked pulling her handkerchief out of her mouth.

"You little crazy bastard, you don't think anyone's going to notice we're missing?" Mom shouted groggily through her tears. She tried to move but Craig had tied her hands and feet to the chair.

"Craig, my momma don't have nothing to do with this. Why would you taser her?"

"I don't know, maybe because you played me like a fool. Renee, you know this kid Omar?"

"Craig, you're being ridiculous," I interrupted.

"I'm being honest. I'm being real. Brea told me we were getting back together. So I waited but all I got was a visit from the cops."

"Craig you're not thinking clearly. Please calm down," mom begged.

"I'm not your son, you can't tell me what to do. You always up in somebody's business. My daddy's in jail because of you," he said angrily, slapping her to the ground.

"Momma," I screamed trying to stand up, but he tied my feet to the chair and my hands behind my back.

He picked her up and threw her back into the chair ignoring me.

"Excuse me Ms. Boyd, no disrespect, I didn't mean to mess up your perfect hair," he said rubbing his fingers through her hair.

"Leave her alone please! You're acting crazy!" I begged. "What do you want Craig?" I screamed trying to get him to leave my mom alone.

By now both our phones were ringing off the hook, but Craig just kept pacing and getting angrier.

"See Brea, this is what I'm talking about," he said snatching my phone and reading my message.

"Brea, pick up, I'm worried about you..."

"I'm gone hurt him. He think he can call my woman and check on her? Naw, that ain't happening! I'm going over there as soon as I'm finished here," he continued while pacing the floor. I didn't say anything because when he gets this angry there's no reasoning with him.

Suddenly, he stopped pacing and pulled out a bottle from his pocket.

"Oh my God, what's that? Please Craig, don't hurt my mom I'll do anything you want," I begged.

"Shut up Brea and I mean it," he said walking close to my face.

"Did you hear me? Shut your lying mouth right now!"

"I'm sorry Craig, I was scared. Can you try to see it from my point of view," I tried to explain.

"Don't beg him for anything!" Mom screamed.

"Listen to your momma Brea. Ain't that what you always do anyway? Renee, I can't stand you because you always sticking your nose into other people's business," he said walking up to her.

"Yeah you just kept on until Detective Daniels found what he was looking for. You're the reason my whole life has changed," he said pouring the liquid on the towel and putting it over my mother's face.

She was yelling and crying and then all of a sudden she slid down the chair. I was screaming and begging him not to hurt her.

"She ain't who you need to be worried about," he explained turning to face me.

He kneeled down to untie my feet.

As he untied me, I noticed he had a gun.

"Craig, is that a gun?" I asked in horror.

"Oh baby, don't be scared," he said kissing me on my forehead. "Will you marry me," he asked touching me on my body.

Tears were rolling down my face because here I was again at the mercy of this crazy man.

After untying me, he stood me to my feet.

"Why you do me like that Brea? Let some other dude touch on you."

"Craig, this has nothing to do with him, he aint' nobody. This is about me and you and I know we can figure out how to work this out. I promise if you let me and my momma go, I won't tell anyone."

"See Brea, you don't understand me. I can't let you go. You're my heart. You're my life and I think about you day and night. Naw, I'm never giving you up," he said pulling my arm.

"Let's go," he said picking me up walking outside.

"Craig, where are you taking me? What about my mom?"

"We'll be back. I have a surprise for you."

"I wanted to take you on a boat ride," he said walking me down the long pier where my mom and Aunt Sandra kept their fishing boat.

Neither one of them could actually fish or swim, but they kept it so they could take pictures to send to their friends on MyBook. I wished she didn't have a boat now.

"It's cold out here, please can we go back in the house," I said while crying. He dragged me to the end of the pier and sat me down.

"Now look Brea, you need to stop all this fighting," he explained climbing in the boat to untie it, breathing hard.

"Why we have to get on the boat? Why can't we just talk here," I continued begging.

"Because I want to ride on the boat. I'm getting ready to bring your boy Omar with us," he said sarcastically.

I knew if he got me on that boat, my mom would never see me or him alive again.

While he was getting the boat ready, I noticed this time when he tied me up he was so busy trying to get him a feel, he didn't tie me very tight, so I knew if I could just wiggle loose I could run.

My plan was to try and get to the house and help my mom.

He picked me up again to try and throw me in the boat but I started sitting down and making him drag me. In the struggle, the ropes came off.

This was my chance to get away. I ran to the door for dear life screaming all the way.

"Momma, help me!" I shouted running as fast as I could.

He was close behind, and by now I knew he was going to catch me.

When I felt him on my heels, I stopped and dropped to the ground which made him trip over me and fall into the water. When he fell in the water, I started running again.

By then my mom had started crawling out of the door. He climbed out of the water screaming.

"Brea, why are you acting like this? I just want to take you on a boat ride. You used to love doing things like that with me," he said running toward the door.

"Oh look, mommy's up, I should've given her more medicine," he said laughing.

I was almost at the end of the pier when my mom screamed my name.

"Brea, run!" she said faintly.

I heard a loud bang and me and my mom both covered our ears and I fell to the ground. I felt all over my body screaming to see if he had shot me.

"Dang Brea, you pissing me off," he said grabbing me off the ground. He'd shot the top of the door.

"That was a warning shot," he said grabbing my arm. I made up my mind I was going to fight for my life. I slapped him with my other hand and started scratching him.

He swung at me and missed and that's when I kicked him between the legs.

When he hit the ground, I took off running again. I was maybe 10 feet away from my mom when I heard him cock the gun again. I froze and put my hands in the air.

Suddenly, I heard a loud crack again and this time everything went blank.

I felt like you feel just before you fall asleep. You know you're sleep but you're still conscious. I could feel tears rolling down my face, but I couldn't wipe them. I felt a strong wind sweep past me and I could hear Craig and my mom struggle.

The longer I laid there, the sounds began to fade away and my mind went back to when I was a little girl dancing. I could see myself in my pretty pink dress twirling around and standing on my toes. It took me years to learn to get "on point" in ballet.

I'd loved dancing since I was little girl, and this time when I saw myself dancing, I was on Broadway.

"Brea," I could faintly hear my mom yelling. I could hear sirens and people running, but I was dancing.

For the first time since I met Craig, the noise stopped and I didn't feel scared anymore.

"Is this purgatory? Am I dead?" I thought to myself.

I felt my body being lifted as someone kept shining a bright light into my eyes. I wished I could wake up to tell him how annoying he was being.

I came to when a pain ran through my head which made me sit straight up. The paramedics were all around me and my mother was crying. I didn't know where I was or what was happening because my head hurt so badly.

I was screaming and crying when I fell back on the gurney realizing what Craig had done to me. While I stood there with my hands in the air begging him for my life, he shot me in the head.

The man who had made so many promises and made me so happy did what I always feared he'd do, he tried to kill me.

I don't remember much about the incident after that. I was in ICU for two days and doctors kept coming in my rooming staring at me and saying what a miracle I was.

It didn't take me long to breathe on my own and after tons of MRI's they let me go home after one week.

My nurse came in to discharge me and told me how close I came to dying. She was African and had a really funny accent.

"You're blessed child," she kept saying over and over again.

My mom and dad had been at the hospital nonstop since I'd been admitted and they cried every time they looked at me.

I felt blessed because I lived and I finally felt strong because even after Craig had thrown his best punch, he didn't break me.

I took over Lois' nightly text because I had to share with everyone how good God is and how He'd saved my life.

Physically, I'll never be the same again. The bullet hit me in the brain where the doctors couldn't operate. That means I have a bullet stuck in my head for the rest of my life.

My forehead has a small scar that reminds me everyday of what I went through. I have small seizures which causes everyone to cry, and I can't get too stressed or move too fast.

The only other problem is the migraines that come unannounced which cause me to have to be in the dark with all the blinds closed. Sometimes it hurts so bad I cry.

It's during these times that I understand just how good God is. Feeling the pain reminds me that I'm alive and I can't help but be happy about that.

I'm not the same Brea anymore but I'm a better Brea because I found myself, even in the midst of the terror. I knew God had saved me, because I wasn't supposed to live and if I did, I wasn't supposed to be able to walk or talk.

It took me a few days to clearly understand what had happened and how Craig got caught.

I found out my mom saved both of our lives. When Craig walked pass me, he had the gun pointed at her. As he got closer, she reached out and tasered him and he fell down backwards on the porch and knocked himself out.

The security guard, Big Walter, found Dr. Lewis lying in the parking lot and he called the police. They got in touch with Tiffany who told them I was missing and with everything that had been happening with Craig, the police came right away. By the time Craig came to, he was handcuffed in the back of a police car.

Since that day, Omar has never left my side. I thought maybe he stayed around because he felt guilty about not walking me to my car, but if that's the reason, he tried hard to hide it.

After all that, I finally had the strength I needed to testify in court against Craig about what he had done to me and my mom.

He was sentenced to ten years in prison. They added another two for the kidnapping and general arrogance.

His father was eventually found guilty of murdering his mom as well. I thought the only true justice was for both of them to be in a cell together.

The news reported he drugged Mrs. Lyles because she was getting ready to expose him for beating her and money laundering. She would've walked away with more than half of his money.

Shortly after Craig went to jail, I wrote him a letter.

Dear Craig:

I know this letter probably comes as a surprise to you but I've wanted to write you for awhile now. I practiced a few times before these words came to me.

Craig, you were my heart and I loved you so much. I'm angry that you took my trust and love for you and used it to hurt me. I could have died because of you, but God had another plan for my life.

Thank you for the good and the bad times. At first, I couldn't understand how it could be possible, but I'm the woman I am today because of you. No more is the girl who let others step all over her.

You told me one time that you had changed, but now I'm telling you that my life is not about what's happening to you. But the change is in me.

I want you to know that I forgive you Craig for what you did. It's time for you to forgive yourself. I pray you have a wonderful rest of your life.

Stay Lifted,

Brea

That was the end of Craig and me. Even though he was the most romantic boy I'd ever met, his heart was filled with pain and he took it out on me. My love couldn't change him and he preyed upon me and forever changed the course of my life.

Omar and I got married a year after I graduated from college. He was drafted to play professional football and we moved to

Denver. My mom came with us because I began to have children and needed her help.

Tiffany stayed and finished college. After graduation, she took a job in the special events center of the school.

Brad and Lois moved to Italy because Brad was stationed there, so we talk to them all the time on the computer.

My injuries prevented me from ever dancing on Broadway. I could still dance, but the nightly shows would be too grueling. So instead, I used my gift to open a dance school for inner city girls. We travel around the country doing a dance called, "I'm Free." The dance paints the picture of what happened to me, and how I escaped Craig's grip.

Several years after Craig went to jail, I used to think I'd see him everywhere but not until now, this moment did I realize the man who almost killed me twice was actually walking past my car window.

I thought he could hear my heart beating through the door, but he passed the car without even noticing me. As I took a deep breath and peeked through my side mirror, my husband walked out the store holding up my 'Peanut Patty.' I smiled a trembling smile of approval at him while closely monitoring where Craig was. As he climbed in the car, I hugged him like I'd never hugged him before.

He looked at me strangely and started the car. As we road away into our future, I glanced back one last time to say goodbye to my past.

UrbanGirlz, Inc. is an award winning online community dedicated to educating, inspiring and celebrating urban girls and teens.

UrbanGirlz also conducts Community Impact Programs which include the UrbanGirlz National Etiquette Initiative, the Ladies by Design Junior Debutante Course, and UrbanGirlz Resource Central which provides materials for schools, churches and community organizations.

Check out UrbanGirlz resources and materials at www.urbangirlz.org and sign up for our email list.

To contact UrbanGirlz, Inc., P.O. Box 3641, Cedar Hill, Texas 75106 or call 1.800.291.6492.

UrbanGirlz Publishing Titles

Non-Fiction
10 Strategies to Success for Urban Teenz
Urban Etiquette Teenz Series
Bible Basics Resource Guide
Starting Your Etiquette Business
Ladies by Design Junior Debutante Course

Fiction
The Designer's Daughter

Get ready for Book #2 in the UrbanGirlz Street Series
Maid Rich – *Release date: June 2011*

Kylah looses her parents, home and money. She goes from riches to rags to a whole new life.

For Help Call the National Domestic Violence Hotline

(800) 799-7233

www.ingramcontent.com/pod-product-compliance
Lightning Source LLC
Chambersburg PA
CBHW051251170626
46809CB00004B/1596